Donald Windham

TWO PEOPLE

EX LIBRIS: DONALD WINDHAM

NOVELS

The Dog Star, 1950
The Hero Continues, 1960
Two People, 1965
Tanaquil, 1972
Stone in the Hourglass, 1981

STORIES

The Warm Country, 1960

PLAYS

You Touched Me!, 1947 (with Tennessee Williams)
The Starless Air, 1953

MEMOIRS

Emblems of Conduct, 1964
Lost Friendships, 1987
1948: Italy, 1998

TWO PEOPLE

A Novel by
DONALD WINDHAM

MONDIAL

Mondial
New York

TWO PEOPLE

A novel by
Donald Windham

First edition published by Coward-McCann, Inc., 1965.

Cover: *Other* (1981). Collage by Fritz Bultman.
Pasted paper and gouache, 52″ x 46″.
Reproduced by permission of Jeanne Bultman.

ISBN 978-1-59569-103-3
Library of Congress Control Number: 2008938595

www.mondialbooks.com

To

FRITZ and JEANNE
BULTMAN

CHAPTER 1

A number of people jumped from bridges into the Tiber yesterday. Forrest saw the item in a newspaper lying on the projecting terrace of the Pincio.

Their intention, it turned out, was diversion, not suicide. The newspaper was a month old and jumping into the Tiber is a Roman way of celebrating the New Year.

He turned away from the Pincio terrace and entered the park. Ahead of him, beneath the obelisk in the center of Viale dell'Obelisco, two boys wearing pale blue coveralls inscribed with the name of a garage were teasing two girls dressed in the white uniforms of a hairdressing establishment. All four were beautiful, but in the encounter the girls suffered the disadvantage of having to play their parts with frowning disapproval, while the boys, each with an arm around the other's neck, and holding hands in the pocket of one of their coveralls, laughingly threw themselves before, between, and behind the girls. Like true sportsmen, they enjoyed the game more the greater the opposition of their adversaries. They switched direction whenever the girls did. The procession, continually turning on itself, came back toward Forrest each time it went a short way ahead of him. Then it was four o'clock. The girls marched off in one direction; the boys, holding onto each other, reeled off in the opposite.

Forrest followed the girls toward Trinità dei Monti. At the top of the Spanish Steps, he leaned on the balustrade and watched the girls descend. It consoled him to look at the Spanish Steps. The church of Trinità dei Monti, behind him, had been there first, at the top of the hill; at the bottom, Piazza di Spagna and the low fountain. The architect had come into this disordered landscape and given it a center so perfect that it was difficult to believe that the surrounding constructions had not grown up around the steps. How satisfying it would be, he thought, to fit so well into your situation that your presence seems to have produced it.

As Forrest leaned there, wondering what he was going to do, he caught sight of a black-haired boy in a white raincoat coming up the steps toward him. He had seen the boy once before, in the same place. He had been standing at the balustrade with Robert, a travel representative for an airline, in whose apartment he was staying. Robert was an old friend of Forrest's wife. Forrest had met him upon their arrival in Rome when Robert, who was being transferred to Athens, had offered to sublet them his apartment. They had agreed to take the apartment and moved in. Then Forrest's wife had gone back to the States and left him alone.

He remembered the black-haired boy in the white raincoat because that first day the boy had frowned and stopped in his tracks when he caught sight of Forrest. He walked on after an instant, disappearing into the last flight of steps, and reappeared soon afterward at the end of the balustrade. His frown was the sort that can come from self-consciousness but that can also come from ill temper, and in his case it looked like ill temper. He walked slowly past, then stopped in front of the obelisk that rises at the top of the Spanish Steps, like the obelisk in the center of the Pincio. After a minute, he turned toward Forrest and Robert and gave them a long look.

"Is that a friend of yours?" Forrest asked. And Robert, glancing at the boy, replied:

"No, I've never seen him before." Forrest had often seen Robert talking to boys at the Steps. He had met one or two of the boys leaving the apartment. Robert did not talk about his friendships, but he made no effort at concealment. And Forrest, although similar conduct was accepted by the people he knew in New York, was surprised to find that here with these young Romans it had no hint of limitation or perversion. He was curious and impressed by how pleasantly Robert lived, as though the ambient air of Rome, with its innocent male conviviality, gave a more permissive aspect to this activity. In any case, Robert was an embodiment of his profession: whomever he went to bed with, there was no hint that he had any permanent attachment in Rome. His directness gave him the air of meaning exactly what he said and no more. One day he had said to Forrest that promiscuous encounters are to Italian boys what ice cream sodas at the corner drugstore are to their American counterparts. Forrest considered this an extreme opinion, but he had no grounds on which to contradict it. The boy in the white raincoat was the first that he had mentioned to Robert.

The boy had seemed in a hurry while he was walking that first day. When he stopped, a look of business and purpose still separated him from the aimless people around him. His immobility was a deliberate move; it entirely lacked the gracious air, so nearly universal among the young workmen and students Forrest had seen on the Steps, of their being there for their own diversion, to pass their own free time, regardless of the form that the passing of it might take.

"I've seldom seen a Roman frown like that," he said.

"A Roman usually doesn't," Robert replied. "He's probably from Florence."

The boy had been watching them when they walked on. But it was less the boy than it was the conversation that Forrest had had with Robert at dinner in the evening that made him remember the day so well.

Robert had taken him to a small trattoria on Via di Ripetta. They entered past a long table loaded with artichokes alla Romana; stuffed tomatoes; platters containing tiny clams in their shells; spiedini of sausages, livers, laurel leaves; and every kind of roast meat, poultry, and game. The trattoria had no menu. As soon as they sat down, the waiter rattled off a list of other dishes available that day. The Italian ideal, Robert added, was to think up some pasta or other concoction besides those offered and give precise instructions for its preparation.

"I came here last year on Befana with three Englishwomen," Robert said toward the end of the meal. "Afterward, we went to Piazza Navona to watch the crowd. My friends all wore their hair cut short and one had a small mustache. The children kept circling around them, asking for presents. They thought that they were disguised as witches."

Forrest laughed.

"They must have been furious."

"On the contrary. They were delighted. They'd never been such centers of attention before."

"That's surprising, from the way you describe them."

Robert pushed away his fruit plate and gave Forrest a look.

"Rome is full of surprises."

"What do you mean?"

"It was here that your wife left you."

Forrest, disconcerted, reached for a cigarette before he remembered that he had stopped smoking.

"That had something to do with Rome, didn't it?"

"Perhaps. She said that Rome made her nervous. But she'd said that about most of the places we'd been."

"I hope it didn't have anything to do with me."

"Of course not."

"Well, wives have a way of being annoyed if their husbands don't like their old friends, and just as annoyed if they do. Also, it can be difficult for a couple to share an apartment with a third person, even for a few days."

"She enjoyed seeing you. Our troubles started much earlier."

"And I didn't bring them to a head?"

"No."

"I'm glad. Perhaps, as I said, it's just that Rome is full of surprises."

"I hope so. I really don't know what happened between us. Maybe she just wanted to get back to the children. Anyway, I'm sure that everything will work out all right."

"Good. Maybe Rome will take care of it, in its round-about way."

It had rained while they were eating. The rain had stopped, and Robert suggested that they walk to Piazza Navona. As they went, Forrest tried to say clearly in his mind what had happened between him and his wife. It was difficult. His memory of their discord was like the memory of a conversation where one person says "What?" and the other replies with the same word. The first explains, "I didn't say anything, I was asking what you said." The second objects, "I didn't say anything." And the first, "Oh, I thought that you did."

They had argued from the beginning of their holiday in Europe. At first, his wife had blamed it on his having been ill and on his having given up smoking. Their arguments seldom originated from anything that either of them cared about. The discord came from within, but it was momentary and petty difficulties that called it out. In England, where they had more acquaintances and the life was more famil-iar, there were only minor disturbances. They were suffi-ciently in control of the situation when things went wrong to surmount their annoyance or to turn it on outsiders. The situation became worse, however, as soon as there were mysteries of language and custom. In France, it was easier for them to be nonplussed by the behavior of taxi drivers and waiters. They blamed each other for not taking the initiative in difficulties, then both assumed command of the situation, or resigned it to the other, at the same moment.

In Italy, her need to stand between him and new experiences — which worked fairly well at home — did not work at all. How deeply she needed to do this was recalled to him by something that had happened before they left the States. He had gone into a drugstore one day when they were packing and bought tubes and bottles of all the pharmaceutical products that they used. As they were traveling on a boat and were to be away a long time, he bought the large size of each. She took them all back the next day and changed them for smaller sizes. It seemed a pointless opposition, yet pointless to argue about, and he let it go.

By the time they reached Rome, communication was impossible between them when something went wrong. Suddenly, they had to repeat the simplest sentence, to explain the simplest story, to elaborate the simplest statement. One of them would not know what the other was talking about although it was the same thing that they had been talking about a moment before. Communication short-circuited, and they no longer were able to fall back on the ordinary explanations used by people who have not lived together for eight years.

Forrest wished that they had disagreed over Robert, or over something specific. It would have been a help if a distance had come between them. But without the children and without his work they were too close together, not too far apart. The week that Robert was in Milan and they moved into the apartment, each day ended in a fight. The trouble began as the daylight faded. He lit the fire of wooden logs in the front room. She mixed drinks. They sat down, believing that everything would be all right and that they would have a pleasant evening. Misunderstanding came as suddenly as the Roman air changes from warm to cold as you step from sun to shade. The conversation split in two. Humor, friendliness, civility vanished. His wife said that she had told him something that he had not heard. That was possible. Then she said that he had made a statement that he had not made. That was impossible. Soon, each was staring into the fire, saying things that would be regretted. And one morning she had announced that she was returning home.

Befana, the eve of Twelfth-night, when Italian children receive their presents, is a combination of Halloween and Christmas. Piazza Navona was as crowded as though it had not rained. The light-strung toy stands set up around the long stadium-shaped piazza were crowded with customers; the shouting torrone venders were doing a good business. The din was terrific.

Forrest and Robert found themselves pressed so closely in the slowly revolving mob that it was impossible to avoid having whistles blown directly in their ears. A group of boys, grinning furiously to show that their intentions were friendly, pounded them over their heads with sponge-headed hammers. Forrest, feeling the same homesickness that he had felt at Christmas, pushed his way to one of the stands and looked at the toys displayed. His two little girls did not care much for dolls, but they were fond of anything to do with animals; and here were cats riding tricycles, elephants driving trains, dogs tending bar. When he had bought two of the toys and turned to look for Robert, he saw him near the Fontana del Moro at the end of the piazza, talking to the boys with the sponge-headed hammers.

As Forrest came up, the boys were passing Robert's notebook from hand to hand, writing their names and telephone numbers in it.

"They say that we are sympathetic foreigners," Robert explained, "and that they want to be our friends."

Each of them introduced himself to Forrest. One of them suggested that they accompany Forrest and Robert for the evening. Robert declined the offer.

"I hope that you didn't want to bother with them," he added to Forrest when they were walking again.

"Either way."

"In any case," Robert said, tearing the page out of his notebook, "I'll give you this. I go to Naples tomorrow. When I come back, I'll be leaving for good. And it might come in handy for you."

"What for?"

"They could be useful at showing you around sometimes." Robert held out the piece of paper. "Take it."

"I've decided to leave Rome, too," Forrest said. "I don't think, after all, that I want to stay on here alone."

"At least stay until the quarter's rent is up. You've paid me and I've paid the landlady, and we'll never get anything back out of her."

"Don't you know someone that you'd like to give the place to?"

"I can't hear you," Robert shouted over the blast of a horn. "Let's get out of here and go somewhere quiet for a coffee."

In the narrow street that led off the piazza, Forrest crumpled up the notebook page and dropped it. He did it quickly, where it was dark; but when they were around the corner, instead of finding the bar that Robert was looking for, they entered a section where the electricity had failed. The effect was in complete contrast to Piazza Navona, and in contrast to most things that Forrest had seen in Rome. Since his arrival, the city had struck him as familiar and unreal. The traveling Luna Parks. The earth-colored buildings. The endless traffic jams. The businessmen with liverish faces. His quarrels with his wife. Despite the ruins and monuments of Vecchia Roma, he missed the sense of the past that he had expected. The familiarity was modern and nervous, and he had been impressed, even in the poorest quarters, by the absence of medieval darkness and mystery. Suddenly, with an intensity that made the hairs of his neck stand on end, he was in the midst of it. A century separated him from the shops and buses of the Ludovisi quarter. Candles shone on tables inside a small trattoria. In the dark narrow space between the high walls of the street, sounds carried with an extraordinary sharpness. The voice of an unseen youth in a doorway, calling "Avanti, vieni qua!" seemed to come from lips almost touching Forrest's ear. The girl's laughter that answered was innocent and intimate. He and Robert and the girl were all making their ways up the street. There had been a garbage collectors' strike for several days and rubbish, thrown from doors and windows of the buildings, had not been collected. As they neared Campo dei Fiori, something soft and wet squish-squashed beneath Forrest's shoe. The youth's call was repeated in the doorway ahead, answered by the girl's laughter and by a harsher voice from above. Looking up, Forrest saw a line of washed clothes silhouetted against the sky with an umbrella propped above to protect them from the rain.

The morning after the evening that he had first seen the black-haired boy in the white raincoat and had gone to Piazza Navona with Robert, he spent surrounded by the musty volumes of the Biblioteca Vittorio Emanuele. Disappointingly, the books did not give him as strong a sense of the past as he had had the night before, but he stayed in the library until lunch-time. Following his wife's departure, finding himself with nothing to do much of the time, he had decided to fill part of his days by searching out documents on the last years of the life of Giordano Bruno, the Dominican who was burned as a heretic in Campo dei Fiori in 1600, and who had been the subject of Forrest's thesis when he was at Columbia, majoring in history and not yet thinking of marrying and becoming a broker.

Since his marriage, he was not used to being alone. In New York, his days were as full as the briefcase he carried to work each morning and as much alike as the business suits he wore. Twice a week, he played handball after he left the office; about as often, he and his wife had guests to dinner or called a baby sitter and ate at the house of friends. But he never found himself alone with time on his hands. When he had first come to New York from the Middle West, he had felt that living in Manhattan was like being at a party given by rich and interesting people whom he knew only slightly. He missed his family's house, full of brothers and sisters, and he could not get used to living alone in one room. He looked on the city with round, friendly eyes, whose irises exactly touched the tops and bottoms of their openings; but his amiable disposition was combined with a shyness that made him slow in making friends. This problem disappeared when he fell in love with his wife. He spent as much time with her as possible. Her large circle of friends—business acquaintances of her father's, among whom she had met him, actors and writers—became his. Then there were the children.

The sparsity of his days in Rome, compared with their plentitude in New York, had taken on a baffling quality that brought to his mind the Italian word for *nothing: niente*. The slide of its nasal syllables, pronounced by Italians as an answer to almost any question that they did not care to discuss further, turned *nothing* into a reality as formidable as a day of twenty-four hours stretching before him with no appointments, yet with no chances for his fulfilling its opportunities. *Niente* was not merely blank, as his days had been during the months he was sick in bed with hepatitis. And it was not merely weak, as he had been after he went back to work and began to buckle under the pressure. *Niente* was the intangible barrier that by some negative means, now that he was well and strong, shut him out from the intimate Roman life that he saw Robert and others enjoying, just as loneliness had shut him out from New York life before he was married.

The Biblioteca Vittorio Emanuele was a makeshift for the research he wanted to do. He had inquired shortly after his wife left for a permit to use the Vatican Archives. But if he was not going to stay long in Rome he could not count on receiving it before he left. He might as well settle for these state libraries which were more accessible. Nevertheless, he did not cut short the effort he had started to obtain the permit. The second evening after his walk in the dark near Campo dei Fiori, he went to dinner at the house of a friend who had arranged for him to meet an American cardinal who could give him the recommendation he needed for the Vatican permit.

The weather, following the shower on the night of Befana, had turned to the kind described in dispatches from Rome as "partly cloudy." The sky was black on and off all day. Storms rained themselves out and started again hourly. In between, it thundered. The sun came out by late afternoon. While Forrest was dressing, there was a magnificent sunset. The clouds cleared. The moon rose. Then, at the moment he started out, a downpour filled the streets with water up to the tops of his shoes.

His hostess lived in a small street of new buildings near Piazzale delle Medaglie d'Oro. The bus that he took crossed the river and started up a long tree-lined street with a lighted fountain in the distance. On the other side of the fountain, it twisted up a hill into the dark, as though leading into the country. Then blocks of new apartment houses appeared.

Forrest had explained on the telephone that his wife had gone back to the States, but he was forced to repeat his explanation as he was taking off his raincoat in the vestibule. His hostess listened carefully, then took his hand, patted it, and led him into the room to introduce him to the other guests.

After dinner, the cardinal told him that if he was allowed to see unpublished documents about Giordano Bruno in the Archives, which was unlikely, and if they were legible, which was more unlikely, they would be in such bad Latin that unless he was an optimum scholar of the vagaries of medieval Latin, most unlikely of all in a non-Catholic layman, he probably would be unable to read them. The cardinal's series of warnings was given jovially, with smiles, almost with laughter. It ended in an offer to find him, if he wished, a gifted, unprejudiced young student of theology who knew his way through the Porta di Sant'Anna and would help him. Then he gave Forrest the recommendation.

He mailed it the next day, together with a letter to his wife saying that he thought he would leave Rome and asking if he should return to New York. Afterward, he went back to his books in the government library. They kept him pleasantly in motion. The Biblioteca Nazionale is in several buildings scattered about the section of Vecchia Roma, full of ecclesiastical stores and cats, that is near the Pantheon. He went from one to another, dodging showers. Nothing abruptly decisive happened. He did not progress fast enough to accomplish anything if he left Rome soon. A book that he asked for might be ready if he went back in twenty-four hours. If it was not, he went back in forty-eight. The chances of his receiving it then were about the same as his chances of arriving where he was going before it rained — fifty-fifty.

Several unpleasant surprises awaited him at the apartment in the evenings. The first was an answering letter from his wife. When she had left he had felt sure that she wanted him to go with her. Now she wrote that they should remain apart. And he admitted to himself that he was afraid to return. He did not believe, as he had said to Robert, that everything would work out all right. He resented that their fights had ruined Rome for him, and he felt that if he went back with nothing changed there would be no more for them in marriage as they had known it. But it upset him to know that his wife felt the same way. Instead of trying to get back their apartment in New York, she had told the people who had sublet it that they could keep it for the original six months. She would stay with her parents in Southport, where the children had been all along. After that, they would discuss what would happen.

He did not eat that night. The depression returned that he had experienced during the evenings of discord when they were in Rome together. He had skipped dinner the evening before, because he did not have an engagement and did not feel like eating alone. Remembering this, he went out with the letter in his pocket and walked around. But he could not make up his mind to enter any of the restaurants that he passed. He ended by ascending the steps from Piazza del Popolo to the Pincio and crossing the Villa Borghese to Via Veneto where he drank a negroni standing at the counter of a bar. After two drinks, he knew that he should go out and eat or he would be drunk. But when he was outside again, the idea of food was no more possible than before.

He missed the apartment in New York. It was a clutter of large and small rooms, perhaps unimpressive in comparison with the apartment he was occupying in Rome; but he wished that he could sleep there that night. His wife must no longer love him if she had not wanted to return there. All their happiness was associated with it, and the seemingly useless small rooms had come into their own after the children were born. They had even been able to close up one of them, full of toys, clothing, and mementoes, when they prepared the apartment for subletting. And it depressed him further to think that strangers might have gone into that room, too.

He drank caffè latte in the morning and tried to make a telephone call to his wife. The operator said that the connection would go through in the early evening, about the same hour that he had received the letter the day before. At lunchtime, he was not hungry and did not eat, hoping that abstinence would stimulate his appetite and make him hungry at dinner. He walked by the river, crossing it first on Ponte Sant' Angelo, then recrossing it on Ponte Garibaldi. The idea of jumping in did not tempt him; nevertheless, the water viewed from the bridges suited his mood. He spent a long time standing at the top of the Spanish Steps, looking at the pools of rain in the dark sponge-holes of the travertine. When he returned to the apartment, he collected all the small rugs from the various rooms, put them beneath his feet on the cold terrazzo floor in the dining room, and tried to write a letter while he waited for the call.

It was noon in Connecticut. His wife, ready to go to New York for the day, said that she was sorry that her letter had upset him. Nevertheless, it was better to face facts. He agreed, but when he tried to tell her that the whole difficulty was a misunderstanding, she did not want to listen.

"There comes a point," she said, "when you don't want to be told any more."

"Do you mean that you want to divorce me?"

"No. If I wanted to divorce you, it would solve every-thing. But I don't want to talk about it now."

He asked to say hello to the children. They had gone shopping with their grandmother.

"I sent them some toys last week," he added. "Like the ones we bought them at Christmas, but different. Is your father there?"

"He's in the city. It's noon here, you know."

"Doesn't he think it odd of me to stay on without you?"

"No. I told him that it was more of a rest for you."

"He hasn't written me since you've been back."

"I'll tell him to write. He said that he hasn't heard from you, either."

"I haven't known what to say."

The children were well, his wife added: the older one had lost one of her front teeth and looked funny; the younger had become so fond of a pair of artificial hairbraids that she wore them in bed at night.

"Are you all right?" he asked.

"Yes, everything is all right."

"And you're sure you don't want me to come back?"

"There's no need for you to come back."

"All right. I don't know what I'll do. I'll write. Take care of yourself."

Just before they said good-bye, she added:

"Take care of yourself, too."

The conversation plunged him into a depression that was composed less of thinking than of wandering through thoughts that he had thought before. Eating was as impos-sible as it had been the previous night. He felt no perverse desire to starve himself, but he felt no more need for food than if he were a ghost or an angel. A lightness, almost a weightlessness, buoyed him up; food would have been a deadly weight on it. He went for a walk, trying to connect to the city, telling himself that he had wanted to stay in Rome without his wife. He should enjoy it.

The night was clear and cold, and the dark was comforting. But the wind, touching his cheeks, his brow, his wrists, increased his loneliness.

Three days had passed since he had eaten when, the next afternoon, Forrest followed the two girls down from the Pincio. Standing at the top of the Spanish Steps, he wondered how long he could go without nourishment. He suffered no bad effects; there was not even a growl from his stomach. But there seemed to be no more reason for him to eat than for him to be in Rome. He felt trapped. He had been to the libraries that morning, but he might as well have slept. There seemed, really, no more reason for him to do one thing than another. Perhaps this had been a good thing the last time he had experienced it, after his return from Korea and before he finished college, when he had spent an aimless year in the Village. But at thirty-three his life should be settled. And a few months before, it had been.

He was wearing a cashmere shirt and a Shetland jacket. The warmth of the sun lay across his head and shoulders as intimately as a hand. As he stood there and watched the black-haired boy in the white raincoat coming up toward him, he longed to forget about himself and become a part of the convivial people around him. The boy's unpleasant air of surveying him for a purpose was the same as it had been the earlier time. His expression, once again, was the kind that appears on a person's face when he wants to end an encounter. But once again he acted as though he wanted to start one. When he reached the top of the steps, he walked past Forrest. The sight of his face was replaced by the arched lines of his neck and the childlike shape of his skull.

He stopped at the Pincian end of the balustrade and

looked down the way he had come. Then he glanced from the steps toward Forrest and back again. There was no hint of friendliness in the look. It was a look that accused rather than invited. Something in it, and in its recurrence, annoyed Forrest. He felt trapped enough, cut off from his own life and the life of Rome, without being surveyed this way each time he encountered this boy. Then the boy, his attitude carefully balanced between the indifference of a departure and the deliberateness of an approach, walked past the people between them and toward Forrest in the sunshine. He kept his eyes up, but his expression did not soften or give any hint that a greeting was forming behind it. And Forrest thought: This has gone far enough; I will put a stop to it.

When he spoke, his "buon giorno" had a magical result. He had seen the same effect before, but never to the same degree. The syllables broke an enchantment. The boy's smile changed every detail in his face. All hint of ill temper disappeared. His features became as youthful as the shape of his head. The eyes glowed like the eyes of a child of six. He put both hands to his chest in a gesture like that of a squirrel in Central Park hoping for a nut, and asked:

"Me?"

Forrest was disconcerted. He felt that he had spoken to a different person from the one he had decided to speak to, and he wanted to say the opposite of what he had planned to say. The best that he could manage was:

"It's a beautiful day."

The boy agreed and waited. Forrest asked if he lived in Rome.

"Yes."

"Do you work nearby?"

"I go to school."

"Near here?"

"At Piazza Venezia."

"What do you study?"

"History. Italian. Trigonometry."

He enunciated the words with affable distaste. The two of them stood for a moment, the boy's smile a part of the sunshine. Out of the same sunshine, Forrest heard his own voice asking:

"Would you like to come home with me?"

A shadow passed from Piazza di Spagna, up the white travertine theatre of the steps, and over the obelisk. The boy frowned, then smiled.

"Yes."

Forrest felt a sudden guilt that made him question his intention at the same moment that he became aware of it. Self-conscious, he did not want to descend the steps under the eyes of all the people there. He pointed in the direction of the Pincio and the boy nodded. As they walked beside the wall that runs toward the outdoor café facing the Villa Medici, he asked if the boy studied English. The answer was yes, but the boy would not attempt a word of it. Even in Italian, he only answered questions. He did not ask how long Forrest had been in Rome, if he was married or single, lived in an apartment or hotel, was American or English—none of the Mediterranean questions. And he replied to Forrest's demands with the bare precision of a child responding to a catechism. His name was Marcello. He was seventeen. He had two sisters and a brother. He lived in Monte Mario.

"Piazzale Medaglie d'Oro is in Monte Mario, isn't it?"

"Yes."

"I went there the other night."

The word to *go* is conjugated in Italian with *be* rather than *have* as auxiliary. Forrest knew this, but he usually said it wrong. The boy corrected him. So far from being usual, this was the first time any Roman had ever admitted to him that his broken Italian was anything but perfect. He was delighted. The correction, however, ended the boy's spontaneous remarks. He continued to smile and to answer, but in between he was as silent as he was beaming. The impression he made was so different from the impression he had made a few minutes before, as well as the other day, that Forrest was inclined to believe that there must be some innocent explanation of his boldness. Perhaps someone had pointed him out to the boy for some reason. Maybe this was a further exaggeration of the Italian gregariousness that he did not understand, and when they reached the apartment the boy would be embarrassed or surprised and take his leave in confusion. Or maybe, at the door of the building, he would politely say good-bye, shake hands, and walk away.

As they turned down the steep incline of Via di San Sebastianello and into the far end of Piazza di Spagna, Forrest said:

"There are more Americans every day at the Spanish Steps."

The statement was an unexpected success. The boy's face burst into a smile that equaled his first one.

"Wait until summer!" he exclaimed. "There are more. Many more! More Americans than Italians."

They turned on to a side street in the neighborhood of Robert's apartment. Forrest saw shopkeepers whom he recognized and was once more embarrassed. At the building, without a word, the boy followed him inside and up the four flights of stairs. At the sight of the front room of the apartment, with its high white walls and transparent-draped windows, its wide expanse of modern and antique furnishings, the boy gave one more expression of unguarded enthusiasm. Then he stopped, as though remembering that this was something that he did not do. On Forrest's invitation, he took off his raincoat and sat down on one of the upholstered chairs that rose like green silk rocks from the terrazzo floor. As Forrest looked at him, sitting there passively with his curved hands lying palms up on his knees, he could think of nothing to say. The boy had retreated into the air of a child paying a visit with adults, resigned to wait until the adults finish their business. He looked alone rather than ill at ease, as though he might be in a doctor's foyer or a train station, with no relation between him and anyone else who happened to be there. There was no longer any hint of either the defiance or the delight that he had shown in the sunlight at the top of the Spanish Steps. His face was serenely beautiful.

Alone before this person whom he did not seem to have seen before or to have any intentions toward, Forrest did not know what to do. His Italian disappeared. He could not even manage the words for: Come and see my room. Instead, he held out his hand. The boy allowed himself to be pulled to his feet and led through the apartment. It was a big apartment. As they walked across the long, bare dining room, Forrest felt more than ever that he had made a mistake, from his viewpoint as well as from the boy's. Obviously, he had started something that he would regret or that would end without anything having come of it. He decided that he might as well get it over with as soon as possible. He sensed, in the sound of their footsteps across the terrazzo floor, the emptiness which he remembered from the promiscuous encounters of his early days in New York when he had found himself alone again so soon that he was unable to believe afterward in the brief series of embraces that separated solitude from solitude. When they reached the bedroom, he decided to be as precipitant as possible. Putting his arms around the boy, he kissed him on the lips. The kiss was returned.

They stood facing one another, Forrest looking at a cluster of freckle-flat moles on one of the boy's cheeks. There was no longer any question of his having been abandoned by his Italian: he had never known the word for undress. He pantomimed pulling his clothes over his head, and once again expected to be opposed. The boy nodded, looked around for a chair, sat down, and began to untie his shoelaces.

The room, the first of two bedrooms, was sparsely furnished: a bed, two chairs, a chest.

When Forrest was in his underwear, he crossed to the bed and turned back the covers. The boy, wearing a short-sleeved brown wool undershirt and white cotton jockey shorts, followed him. He gave a smile and a shiver as he jumped beneath the turned-back covers.

"Are you cold?"

"Only my feet."

Forrest put his feet against the boy's. They were icy. As he pressed them between his own to warm them, he looked down into the brown eyes gazing up at him. Only innocence could be read there.

"In English, we say that someone has cold feet when he is afraid."

The boy nodded.

"Also in Italian."

Forrest pulled his head back and saw that the lips of the face beneath his own were curled up with a hint of amusement. The boy's hands slipped around him, touched the back of his neck, and came to rest lightly on his shoulders.

"We don't need these," Forrest said, throwing back the sheets and blankets far enough for him to remove his underwear. The boy followed suit; then, with another smile and shiver, pulled the covers up close around them.

Forrest dressed while the boy was in the bathroom. He was fully clothed when he watched the Italian get ready to leave. Unself-consciously, the boy removed the robe and slippers that he had borrowed. He pulled on his brown wool under-shirt with slow, precise movements, drew it down under the white jockey shorts and out beneath them at the bottom, to finish by tucking the ends in again under the crotch.

When he had put on his trousers, he sat on the chair and tied his shoelaces as though it were morning and he were at home dressing for school. Then he asked permission to use Forrest's comb and, smiling as though to excuse his vanity, combed his hair at the mirror above the chest.

Forrest watched him, no more sure now than before what sort of person this was. He had heard Robert say that the boys who hung out at the Spanish Steps to be picked up wanted money. But this boy possessed none of the puppy-like characteristics that he had seen in the youths who spoke to Robert, and nothing about him coincided with Forrest's imagination of those boys' characters.

He stood there with his hand on a thousand-lire note in his pocket and wondered if he should give it to the boy. Would he expect nothing? Would he be insulted? Or would he, showing another face that Forrest had not yet seen, threateningly demand a larger sum? Forrest had received so many surprises that one more surprise would not have surprised him. But he had to make up his mind. He fell back on his idea that in no situation is it wrong to offer money to an Italian. When the boy turned from the mirror, Forrest put the bill into his hand.

"May I?"

The boy looked down. Without a muscle in his face moving, a smile came into his eyes. Then he lowered his lids, the smile descended to his lips, and he said:

"Grazie."

He had blushed.

Longing that evening for a friendly, ordinary atmosphere to be in, Forrest remembered the trattoria that Robert had introduced him to. It was run, as Robert had pointed out, by a family. The oldest waiter was the owner. The youngest waiter was his son. There were other hints of a family atmosphere: a dark-faced woman who sometimes poked her head out of the kitchen and a small boy who brought and took away empty plates, making as many mistakes as was possible. Forrest was recognized when he came in. It was early for dinner, just eight o'clock, and all the time that he was there he heard the waiters addressing the arriving clients by name and watched the son joking with a table of soccer players, apparently regular customers, sitting across from him. There was no bill at the end of the meal, as there was no menu at the beginning. The waiter stared at the ceiling, frowned, and announced a sum not much more than half what the food would have cost in most restaurants.

Forrest saw the boy again a week later at the Spanish Steps. He was descending, the boy ascending, and they met on the middle level. After they had talked a few minutes, he asked the boy back to the apartment. His action surprised him, and he tried to reassure himself that what he was doing was unimportant. When he had thought of Robert's going to bed with Roman boys, he had not considered it something that he disapproved of, but something that, as far as he was concerned, there was no point to. Now he remembered an incident that had long been pushed to the back of his mind. When he was a year or two younger than the boy, something had happened that he had never understood. He had been staying at the house of an aunt and uncle in the country. In the middle of the night, his uncle, who had been on a hunting trip, had returned and gotten into bed with him. His uncle's sexual advances awakened him; he was excited and responded. The incident was not repeated.

And neither then nor later was it referred to. He went to the country only occasionally and knew his uncle mainly as the father of several of his older cousins, a convivial man, liked by everyone, who had no noticeable eccentricities. For a long time, Forrest watched him whenever he had a chance and listened to what people said about him, expecting to discover some secret. But he discovered nothing. He was left with what had happened and with his uncle's genial character—and no explanation between them. In the years since, the memory of this had occasionally affected his thinking about other people, but he had not given thought to it in connection to himself. The incident was one of those that do not fit into categories and therefore suggest that categories do not account for everything; but his own life, from the time that he had grown old enough to connect sex with love, had fallen into the most conventional patterns.

This second encounter upset him more than the first. He had not expected to experience again the pleasure that he had felt that earlier afternoon. He considered their meeting a phenomenon, a sport of Rome, not a personal attraction. He could not find a category to put this new desire into, just as he could not fit the boy into any category he knew. The boy's figure, lean and rounded, evoked neither masculinity nor femininity, rather the undivided country of adolescence; and his silent receptivity, open equally to tenderness and passion, spoke of no special desires, but of a need for love so great that it prevented him from asking for it.

That second afternoon, Forrest tried to hide his bewilderment about himself behind his curiosity about the boy. But he could not get the boy to answer any personal questions, and he was unable to retain him after he put on his clothes. With the donning of his garments, the creature who a moment before had seemed removed from all contingencies of time and place, hurried away like any Roman schoolboy with a schedule. During the week that followed, Forrest talked to other youths at the Spanish Steps and to the son at the trattoria. But these efforts had an effect the opposite of that which he wished for. He found these boys perfectly comprehensible, but also perfectly ordinary. He could imagine them doing anything, playing any part, even that of the boy whom he had taken home; and he knew that the counterfeiting of innocence is one of the oldest professions. But what is counterfeited must exist. The imitation has an original. On the other hand, why should he have found the original scowling at him from the top of the Spanish Steps?

Robert returned one morning while a coal-dust-covered giant from a nearby carbonaio shop was filling the carved chest in the entrance hall of the apartment, once a receptacle for some family's silks and brocades, with wooden logs for the fireplace. After greeting Forrest and the maid, whose day it was to clean, Robert put his suitcase down beside the sofa in the front room and announced that he had met an old friend on the plane who would be arriving in a few minutes. He was a director and would be on location in Rome for a week or two, making "postcard" shots for a film. Robert had invited him to stay at the apartment.

Forrest was disappointed that a stranger was to join them. He wanted to tell Robert about the boy, but he was not sure that he would be willing to talk in front of a third person. He could bring up the subject right away, but that would make it seem to have an exaggerated importance, and besides he was put off by the maid's presence. She was an absurdly short and plump and slow woman whose cleaning consisted mainly of circling around the apartment with a dreamy expression on her face as she dusted the tops of valances and doorways with a long-handled feather duster. Instead, he told Robert that he would like to keep the apartment until the end of the quarter, as they had originally planned.

"Apparently no one either wants or expects me back at the moment," he said, "and if I am going to be idle and homeless it may as well be in this apartment."

Robert was delighted. He apologized for having invited the director to stay there, but he had done it in the belief that Forrest would be leaving any day. He immediately telephoned the landlady. A long conversation ensued that consisted, as Forrest found most Italian conversations did, of the same few sentences repeated over and over. At the end, Robert said that the apartment was Forrest's through March. And while he was explaining a few more things about the agreement, the director arrived.

Forrest liked him. He was a Latin American, full of charm and like a lean Italian in appearance. He had been to Italy shortly after the war and he was convinced that the population were all criminals of varying degrees. As soon as he had installed his luggage, he left to see some of the "extortionists" who were arranging his business. He agreed to meet Robert and Forrest for lunch at the trattoria. While they were waiting for him there, Forrest said:

"There's something that I ought to tell you."

"What?"

"Do you remember the boy in the white raincoat that we saw at the Spanish Steps? The one who frowned?"

"Yes."

"I brought him to the apartment the other day."

Influenced, perhaps, by the director's conversation, Robert looked grave.

"Did something unpleasant happen?"

"No, not at all. I just thought that I ought to tell you."

"Well, you don't have to confess to me, you know."

"I'm not confessing. I just want to talk. I didn't under-

stand him at all. He seemed so experienced and yet so innocent."

"You have to remember that Roman boys like to see
new reflections of themselves in foreigners, not the same
ones that they get from their mirrors at home. They talk a
lot, but you can discount most of what they say."

"This one hardly talked at all. He told me that his family
are Sicilians—"

"Sicilians," interrupted the director, who arrived at this
moment, "are the only people in the world more treacher-
ous than Italians. I think that the people I have just left must
be Sicilians."

Forrest was not able to ask the questions he wanted to.
His curiosity remained unsatisfied. But the conversation
probably would not have satisfied it, anyway. Robert left
that evening, looking forward to Greece. Forrest and the
director shared the apartment without difficulty. During
the mornings the next week, Forrest went to the libraries
and to the Salvator Mundi Hospital for liver function tests.
In the afternoons, he often visited the locations where the
film unit was working and watched the crowds who stood
around. Between takes, the director confided to him:

"These people are not looking because they are really
interested. They are used to movie people. It is because they
hope to steal something. Watch the way they look at the
boxes and cables and chairs. Some of them would grab the
camera itself if they had the chance."

Forrest did not see the boy in the crowds, as he had
imagined that he might. Then, one afternoon after he had
given up, he caught sight of him, again at the top of the
Spanish Steps.

It was the last day of carnival. In the Pincio gardens,
hanging above Rome like those of Nebuchadnezzar above
Babylon, the film unit had been photographing color views

of the sun setting behind Saint Peter's. Beneath the trees, young men and women walked around with confetti in their hair. The pale pebbles of the paths between the flower beds were mixed with the many-colored circles of paper. Small bullfighters, Portuguese grandees, gauze-winged bats, Colonial ladies, and Eskimos ran in and out among the flowering azaleas, forsythia, and camellias.

The director and Forrest were walking back toward Trinità dei Monti. It was twilight. Forrest, who had been to the Steps at this time the last few days, had noticed that the streetlights came on three minutes later each evening. He was telling this to the director as they approached the obelisk. The two of them were watching to note the precise moment when the globes of the iron lampposts along the balustrade would be illuminated. They were almost past the boy before Forrest saw him, standing by the balustrade and talking to a man. He had left off wearing the raincoat; his figure was displayed in dark trousers and a crew-neck sweater over the top of which Forrest could see the collar of a pink shirt. Forrest said ciao as they passed. The boy returned the greeting, as one returns the greeting of a casual acquaintance, then went back to his conversation. At the end of the balustrade, Forrest suggested to the director that they stop and look at the view for a moment.

There was a small blue and white airplane travel bag on the balustrade at the boy's side. Forrest wondered if it belonged to him or to the man he was talking to. The man's business suit looked more like an Italian's than an American's, but Forrest was not sure which he was. The director's presence made him self-conscious and he pretended to pay no attention to the couple down the balustrade. Nevertheless, their presence was at the center of his consciousness. He was aware when the boy picked up the airplane bag and he and the man started down the far flight of the Steps together. They paused beside the flower stands when they reached the bottom, then crossed the traffic-filled Piazza di Spagna and turned into the crowd beneath the neon signs of Via Condotti. Once, when they had to step out into the street to pass people on the narrow sidewalk, he saw the man put his arm around the boy and pat him on the shoulder. Via Condotti is straight; its name changes, but it goes on without a turn and diminishes in a direct line, like an illustration in a book on perspective. Forrest could look into it from the top of the Steps all the way to the vanishing point. The two figures grew smaller, disappeared into groups of people, reappeared, then disappeared again, until at last they were lost in the foreshortening of distance, somewhere near the Tiber.

CHAPTER 2

Marcello caught the bus at Porto di Ripetta and got off at Via Andrea Doria. His house was only a short distance farther. The elevator from the lobby rose slowly, emitting the same melancholy squeak that had been his introduction to the building when they had moved in two years earlier.

Claudia let him in the apartment. Without speaking, she pointed at the overcoat on the hook to tell him that their father was home. When he reached the room at the end of the hall that he shared with his little brother, Franco said:

"Papa's home."

"I know."

He threw the airplane bag, containing his gym clothes, onto his bed, took out his school-books, and sat down at the table. But he could not concentrate. He was tired from his workout at the track, and his eyes paid less attention to the trigonometry on the page before them than his ears did to the click of a ball tied to a string that his little brother was tossing into the air and catching in a wooden cup.

"Listen, Franco," he said, going to the chest and taking down a plastic model of a naval destroyer that he had made when they first lived in the apartment. His little brother had coveted it for a long time. "I'll give you this, not just to play with but to keep. But you must take it out into the hall now and let me study in here."

He was not able to concentrate any better when he was alone. He could hear his mother in the kitchen across the hall, preparing supper. The music reached him from the phonograph in his sisters' room, farther away. Then, after a while, his mother called that supper was ready. He heard the drawing back of the chairs as the rest of the family assembled at the table and the click of the glasses and knives and forks as they began to eat.

There was also a dull, chomping sound that he imagined to be his father chewing. He was balancing a pencil on the back of his left hand when the door opened and Claudia came in.

"Lello, Papa says for you to come and eat your supper."

He followed her and stood in the hall doorway. His father demanded:

"Didn't you hear your mother call?"

"Yes."

"Well, sit down."

"You told me to stay in my room at mealtime."

"That was yesterday."

"It was this morning."

"Lello," his mother said, "take your place."

Her eyes pleaded with him to say nothing else. He sat down and began his soup. As he ate, he waited for his father to say something about how late he had arrived home. But the remark did not come. The meal continued in silence, broken only by his mother's directions to his sisters to take away the soup dishes and bring on the other food.

That noon, his father had shouted at the dinner table:

"It is the law of this country that you have to obey me until you are twenty-one. But it is the law that I have to feed you only until you are sixteen. Go to your room and stay there at mealtime."

His mother was afraid to take his side. When he complained to her of his father's picking on him, she answered:

"You may be right that he shouldn't have said that to you. But he is right that you should obey him."

He looked at her now. Her eyes were wary but not unhappy. She looked so much like his father that they might have been brother and sister. His mother put everyone before herself; she wanted to hurt no one, and so was useless as an ally. Even Franco had more power, if he knew how to use it.

"Come here," his father said to Franco at the end of the meal.

Franco marched to the chair at the head of the table. His father leaned forward and nuzzled his neck and chest until he drew back, laughing. Then his father caught him by the shoulders.

"Did you learn to play that game I gave you this morning?"

"Yes, Babbo."

"Come with me and we'll see if you're as good at it as I am."

In his room, Marcello sat down at his table and stared at the trigonometry book, but he could not concentrate any better than he had been able to before. He remembered clearly when his father had loved him. Often, at this hour after supper, he had picked him up, held him in the air above his head, and saying that he was going to eat him alive, had nuzzled him the way he nuzzled Franco. His father hated shopping; he did not supervise the buying of Franco's clothes. But once he had gone with Marcello and his mother to buy him a complete new outfit, including a robin's-egg-blue overcoat, and had made the clerk in the store on Via del Tritone show them the best of everything.

The love had been mutual. When his father's sister was visiting one day when he was small and asked him what he wanted to be when he grew up, he answered:

"A papa."

His father's change of attitude had come before he was aware of having done anything to cause it. It started shortly before they moved out of the old apartment. The first thing he did to cross his father was when he decided to go to the naval school, and at that time he had felt for at least a year that they cared less and less about him at home. That was why he had wanted to go to a school that would take him to the opposite side of the city for most of the day and that would send him into a job away from home as soon as he was graduated.

His awareness of his father's diminishing affection for him was accompanied by his awareness of other things. After the war, they were poor like everyone else. Then, as he was growing up, his father started his own kiln, with a group of Sicilian associates, making tiles for a block of new buildings. The reason for their moving into the new apartment was that it was in a better and more impressive building. But as he became aware of his father's affluence he also became aware of his father's financial meanness. The new apartment allowed his father to impress business associates. But it made life harder for the family. There was not enough space. He and Franco shared the small room across from the kitchen that was supposed to be for the maid. There was no maid. His mother did the work. They ate in a small room so his sisters could sleep in what was supposed to be the dining room. And his father showed off his fancy furniture in the salon.

He and his brother and sisters and mother seemed excluded from the benefits of their increased prosperity. One day he found his mother crying because she did not have the money to pay for a piece of material that she had secretly ordered to make Norma a dress. She was afraid, above all, that his father would find out that she had bought the material after he had said that they did not need it.

"But Papa will know anyway," he said, "when he sees Norma wearing it."

"No, he doesn't notice things so long as he doesn't have to pay for them."

"But he can afford it. Tell him that you know that he has the money."

"No. Your father may have obligations we do not know about. I never question him about his money."

"I will ask him. It is not right for him to make you unhappy."

"No. You must not do that. You can question your father about many things. But you must not question his decisions about money."

That night, he saw that his mother was afraid he would mention the subject before his father. Afterward, he watched and noticed that money was seldom discussed between them. His father really did not question where anything came from or what it cost so long as he was not asked to pay for it. He put a certain sum down on the kitchen table each week, and as long as he was not asked for more he accepted everything.

He paid the fee at the naval school grudgingly. The scholastic standards were high there, yet he treated his son's choice of it with contempt. Marcello supposed that his father wanted him to learn his ceramics business. "Be satisfied to do what your father did or you will come to no good" was a Sicilian saying. His father had never said it to him, yet from the day he started at the school his father acted as though all his expectations were disappointed. Any other school would have been all right, but that one was all wrong. And since he had failed trigonometry at the end of the last term, everything had been impossible.

Obviously, his father's attitude did not come from the school. That was just an excuse. His father had simply ceased to think of him as an object of affection and begun to think of him as a source of income. He had discovered a truth: after a certain age, boys are no longer sons their fathers love but investments they expect to pay off. His father treated him as though he were an employee that he wanted to make a profit on. Yet his father treated the boys at his kiln with more respect than he treated him. It was as though he were an employee who had been hired because he was a relative, one his father would not have had around if he had been left to his own free choice. He felt that his father would not allow him to go on living in the house if his position was one that could be terminated by dismissal. To make up for being unable to fire him, his father tried to control all his activities and to make him do the opposite of whatever he wanted to do. Every conversation hinged on how much he was costing and on what return would come out of the investment. It was a business deal that his opinion had not been asked in, and that he did not understand, but that was all settled. For him, there was no way out.

The door opened. Norma came in. From the way she approached, he knew that she wanted something. She had dark hair like her father and light skin like her mother, but it was her father's character that she shared.

"What are you doing, Lello?"

"Studying."

"Are you coming to the dance with us Sunday?"

"No."

"Why not?"

"I don't feel like it."

"If you don't come, Papa won't let us go."

"I can't help that."

"It's not right of you to take it out on us because you're mad at him."

"I'm not mad at anyone. I have to study. Leave me alone."

Norma, going out, passed Claudia bringing Franco in to put him to bed. His younger sister was the least selfish member of the family. Like his mother, whose light hair she had, she did not want to hurt anyone; but she did not put her father's desires above everything else. She was willing to judge and take sides.

"Untie my shoes for me," Franco said.

"Oh, Franco, you can do it."

But she stooped down and took them off for him.

"Lello," she said when she stood up, "I'm sorry about Papa. But I'm glad that he let you come in and eat."

He grunted a response to her as Norma came back in.

"Papa wants to speak to you, Lello."

"What about?"

"Sunday."

He gave her a furious look as he went out. His father was waiting for him in the salon. The room was filled with many pieces of furniture that contained the tiles his father made. There was even a wood-and-tile Gothic bar.

"You are old enough," his father said, "to think of other people and not of yourself all the time. I don't want you to say anything, but I want you to stop teasing your sisters and to take them to their dance Sunday. Do you understand me?"

"Yes, Papa."

"All right."

When he returned to the back of the apartment his sisters were still in his room and his mother was leaving the kitchen.

"Mamma," he said, "can't you make Norma and Claudia stay in their room? They have a room of their own and they're always in mine and Franco's."

The dance was on Via Andrea Doria, in a building constructed around a court that you entered through an arch from the tree-lined street. Marcello walked his sisters there at twilight. The whole family had been together all day. They had gone to church in the morning, then eaten dinner and visited his father's sister in her apartment near Saint Peter's in the afternoon. For some reason, the regular Sunday dinner fight had not taken place. His father had watched him closely but said nothing. Either the discord of the last few days had released all his disagreeable feelings, or it was enough for him to know that his son was taking his sisters to a dance that he did not want to go to. And, on Marcello's part, it was enough to know that he was outwitting his father. For, despite his refusal to Norma, he had been looking forward to going to the dance, and if his father had known that he wanted to go he would have found some reason to prevent him. He had discovered some time ago that his father watched for his desires in order to have power over him. It was difficult for him to keep silent about his enthusiasms in front of his father; the self-control that was necessary was sometimes too much. But circumstances had taken his side this time.

Norma and Claudia headed straight for the portiera's lodge. He followed them and sat on a chair, talking to the old woman whom all of them had known since they were small, while Claudia put on lipstick and Norma, who had a head cold, removed the woolen petticoat that her father had made her show him that she was wearing before she went out. His sisters, in their way, had learned to get around their father; but it was a way that he disliked. They were incapable of understanding that it was wrong for their father to use his power unfairly. They kowtowed and then disobeyed him behind his back.

Watching them, he understood why men accept the inferiority of women. He almost felt that he had to stand up to his father in order to show his sisters how to behave honorably.

"Tell them not to play the phonograph too loudly," the portiera said. "And not to throw things out of the window."

Her eyes were watering from the cold weather, and her face was so lined that instead of rolling down her cheeks the tears flowed out in little rivers to the sides of her eyes.

"Why are you crying?" Marcello teased her, as they had when they were small.

"Because I haven't a handsome young lover like you."

"Come on," Norma said. "I'm ready. Concetta, we'll be back."

Norma's reason for wanting to come to the dance was that it was the only way she could spend the evening with the boy she was in love with, her fidanzato. As soon as they arrived, she sat down with him on a couch and never danced a step. The parents of the girl to whose apartment they had come had gone to the cinema, leaving them the place to themselves. Most of the couples were doing a step that Marcello did not know. Claudia offered to teach it to him.

"You teach someone else," a girl named Ninì said. "I'll teach Marcello."

He liked dancing with Ninì, although she was not his type. He liked tall girls, and she was very short. He knew her, for she had been in Claudia's class at school for a long time, but she had matured so much recently that he had not recognized her when he saw her at a dance a few weeks before. Perhaps it was the new way she wore her hair, and her voice was lower than his now, so low that it seemed to come from somewhere down near her toes. He thought that she could be a singer.

"I like that shirt you're wearing," she said, glancing up into his eyes and then down at his feet as she showed him the steps. "I noticed it the other week."

Later, when he was not dancing, he watched her across the room, laughing with a group of boys and girls. She was organizing the mixing of drinks with some bottles of vermouth that someone had found. She seemed to be popular. When she glanced in his direction, her eyes passed over him in total indifference, as though she had forgotten who he was, and he decided not to worry over her remark about his shirt. It was a pink Oxford shirt that he had liked when it was new. But it was wearing out, as all his clothes were, and he only wore it with his crew-neck sweater that covered up the threadbare points of the collar.

A boy named Bruno, who lived in Marcello's building, was preparing to take photographs. He had a flash attachment and a high-powered photographer's bulb to put in one of the lamps.

Marcello removed the shade of the lamp. Bruno screwed out the bulb, flicking the room a shade darker, and screwed in the new one. With a flash, the apartment was plunged into darkness.

Everyone cried out. Beneath the voices, the phonograph record slurred to silence. People were bumping into each other. Where is the fuse box? Matches? Candles? A chorus of voices cried that it was better in the dark. Marcello felt alone in the excitement; there was no girl who was his particular friend. Then the lights flashed on and the phonograph record slurred into music.

The glare of the high-powered bulb filled him with energy. He ran around the room, chasing the girl at whose house they were. When the photographs were taken, he posed with his hands held at the top of his head, making rabbit ears. Then he joined a group of his schoolmates who were making plans to go to the soccer match at the stadium the next afternoon.

"Lello, it's nine o'clock," Claudia said.

They went down to the portiera's lodge, then hurried home through the cold, accompanied as far as the door of their building by Norma's fidanzato. Their father was in the salon when they arrived upstairs, entertaining a frog-faced man. Signor Tocci was the manufacturer their father had worked for before he had started his own kiln. Marcello knew that his father hated his former employer; he had often heard him say that the older man was a creature the world would be better off without. At dinner that day, he had said that Signor Tocci was retiring and that someone else would be getting his old customers. Now here he was ingratiating himself. He called his children into the room and introduced them.

"This is my older son, Marcello. You'll remember him from when he was the age Franco is now," he said. "He is studying to be a maritime officer. Marcello, Signor Tocci is the kind of man that admirals are made of."

It was unlike his father to use flattery. Marcello could only assume that knowledge of his own insincerity, and fear that it would show through, made him exaggerate. He watched without mercy as his father begged Signor Tocci to have another glass of Marsala, depreciating the wine that he usually was so proud of and stingy with.

"Yes, I am very fortunate in my children," his father repeated to Signor Tocci, who was childless. "Very fortunate."

And Signor Tocci, smiling with his frog lips drawn back, nodded and said nothing.

Monday, after dinner, on his way to the bus stop to return to school, Marcello ran into Ninì. She was walking along, looking down with a seriousness that was almost matronly on her childish figure, and she did not see him.

"Ciao, Ninì."

"Ciao, Marcello."

"Aren't you going to school?"

She told him that she had quit school before Christmas and was working for her brother.

"Claudia didn't tell me."

"You've probably forgotten. What bus do you take to school?"

"A twenty-three."

"I take a seventy."

"I can take that, too."

As they walked toward the stop, he asked:

"Did you stay late last night?"

"Only a little after you left."

The bus came. It was not crowded, but they stood at the back instead of sitting down.

"It's strange I didn't know you'd quit school," he said. "Where is your family's store?"

"I don't work in the store. My oldest brother has that. I work for my youngest brother in the workshop."

"I didn't know that they had both. They must make a lot of money."

"Yes. They pay me as much as they'd pay a clerk. But I'd rather go to school."

"Have you told them?"

"They know. They don't think a girl needs to be educated."

"My sisters don't want to go to school, but my father makes them."

"There you are."

A feeling of joy rose in him, taking him by surprise.

"Where is the dance next Sunday?" he asked.

"I don't know. A group of us are going to Terminillo to ski, if the weather is right."

"Oh."

"We're going on the auto-pullman, Sunday morning. Why don't you and Norma and Claudia come?"

"I don't think my father will let them."

"Ask him."

"Maybe."

"You ought to come even if they can't."

He did not answer and she said:

"I want to buy some new ski pants, the kind that are waterproof."

"Where do you buy them?"

"From a friend of my brothers'. Near Piazza Vittorio. The stores around here are too expensive."

"I know."

"If you have time, go with me some day. He'll sell them to you at the same price he sells them to us."

The bus was turning into Corso Vittorio Emanuele.

"I have to get off here," Marcello said. "This is the nearest stop to my school. Ciao."

Largo Argentina. Via Paganica. Piazza Mattei. In the middle, the fountain of the tortoises. The fountain is square; at each corner, there is a seashell. Above the seashell, a dolphin; above the dolphin, a nude youth. The youth has one leg with the knee bent and the foot on the dolphin's head; the other leg stretches down to a lower support. One of his hands holds the fish's tail, the other rises above his head to the top basin of the fountain and supports a tortoise.

The four tortoises, except to someone floating in the air above the fountain, or in a window of the surrounding houses, are hardly visible. The main figures are the four youths. Two of them are bare; the other two have fig leaves. Marcello had heard that when the fountain was built for a cardinal in the sixteenth century the sculptor was asked to show the figures for the cardinal's approval. He showed the two with the fig leaves. Then he made the others.

In the sunshine, water fell from several spouts into the white-bottomed pool beneath the seashells. As Marcello passed, bright-colored plastic ice cream spoons were visible on the bottom. His mother had given him his allowance that morning, and as he sat in his history class a few minutes later the images of the bills and coins floated in his mind as clearly as the ice cream spoons had glowed in the basin.

His allowance was only the money necessary for him to take the autobus to and from school twice a day, with a few lire left over. In the past his father had given him other sums, but these had steadily decreased. Recently, his father seemed to expect this thousand-lire-a-week to buy his clothes, also. When he asked for new clothes, his father looked at him and said to wait until his old ones looked worn-out. He and his mother prevented this from happening. But they were able to cover up only in small ways. He had outgrown his last overcoat the winter before; now in cold weather he had only his white gabardine raincoat to wear.

There would be no money for him to go to Terminillo, not even if he walked each day to the cheaper bus stop and did not pay for a print of the photograph that he had promised to buy from Bruno. But he decided to save the money he had planned to use for the soccer match that afternoon. Perhaps something would "happen."

Several months earlier he could have borrowed from the loan society that he had formed with several of his classmates. They were all Lazio fans, who did not like to miss games, and they had met and figured out their scheme in the billiards and ping-pong room beneath the Las Vegas Bar on Via Premuda. Each one gave fifty lire a week. When a member needed money, he could borrow it from the fund. As no one was allowed to borrow for the first month, he had been encouraged by the sight of the thousand lire they accumulated. Loans were to be repaid at the beginning of the week after they were made, with ten percent interest, and he had hoped that there would never be less than a thousand lire in the account. But the first loan was still owing when the second member needed to borrow. As treasurer, he was accused of not having worked out a practical system. But the trouble was that the others were too irresponsible to obey the bylaws. He had discovered another truth: he himself was the only person he could depend on.

The bell for the end of class interrupted his thoughts about money. He took his time accumulating his books and descending the steps from his classroom on the second floor, hoping that he would miss his friends. But they were waiting for him in front of the gymnasium.

"Come on, Marcello. We'll be late."

"I can't go."

"Why not?"

"I have to do an errand nearby for my father."

The others fled toward the stop for the bus to the stadium. He walked in the opposite direction, making his way out of the crowds of boys from the various schools in the vicinity of Piazza Venezia. In a few minutes he entered the long narrow shadow of the Corso.

He should go home and study. Only by making passing grades and being graduated was he going to escape from home. But he was reluctant to return any earlier than necessary to the place where he would encounter his father. At Via Condotti, he turned in the direction of Piazza di Spagna.

Walking slowly, he looked in all the store windows. He was attracted by objects that everyday life had not touched or that it had left behind. The unbought and unused clothes in store displays possessed a quality that he could not name but that he recognized as having seen in the no-longer-used objects in the Ethnological Museum: the feathered vests and sealskin headdresses, the clay pots and ivory hooks and needles. He had not been back to the museum and seen these objects since his school class was taken there nearly three years before, but he remembered the joy he had felt looking into the glass-topped cases. The store windows gave him the same feeling of approaching a pure, unequivocal value that no object managed to retain once it came within the quotidian sphere of being bought and used.

There were special values in the windows on Via Condotti. The prices of the objects were too high, but he saw the originals of the English regimental cravats that he had purchased an Italian imitation of on Via Cola de Rienzo, and authentic Scotch plaid lap robes that looked as though they would be very warm on his feet on cold nights.

Ski pants were in the window of The Sportsman. And a Shetland jacket. After he had looked at them, he crossed the street to the other side and examined the leather bedroom slippers in the window of Arbiter, Son and Man. Then he walked toward the opening of the piazza. He had not consciously thought of going to the Spanish Steps. But as he stood there on the corner there was a break in the traffic and he made his way across the wide-open cobblestone space.

His discovery of sex had taken place at the same time as his discovery of not-being-loved. He had explored the two phenomena simultaneously. The most upsetting part of his discovery about love was his fear that he was no longer capable of loving. He saw none of the failings that his parents saw in him, but this fear, which they showed no awareness of, frightened him so much that it sometimes made him stop in the middle of a gesture.

His closest friend at fourteen was his cousin, Renzo, the son of his father's sister. They lived near Saint Peter's, a few blocks away from his family's old apartment; and although he was not allowed to play in the streets, his father gave him permission to visit his cousin. Under this arrangement, the two of them sometimes managed to escape both their homes.

It was Renzo who initiated him into stealing tomatoes from the gardens off Via Trionfale. Marcello believed in doing what he was told. Until Renzo suggested it, it did not occur to him to make a game of the forbidden. Disobedience did not excite him; but joining Renzo in an adventure did. Renzo dramatized his hunger for a tomato to such an extent the first afternoon that he did not realize that it was not for the tomato but for the excitement of being chased by the people who lived in the shacks above and owned the gardens that Renzo suggested the raid.

Renzo's furtiveness started as soon as they left school. They crawled in the bushes at the side of Via Trionfale, instead of walking up the open incline of the pavement. Then they cut down into the thicker undergrowth beside an opening, filthy with ashes and discarded cans and boxes, where garbage was dumped. Marcello asked why, but Renzo shushed him. The people who lived in the hovels were peasants or squatters, rough people whom Marcello had never had anything to do with. They looked to him as though they would have no restraint if they were angry.

It was the middle of the afternoon, with the sun full out, and when they came into the open they would be visible to anyone who was watching. Renzo suggested that maybe everyone would be asleep. But Marcello did not believe it, and they could see a small child in a dirty dress crawling across the dust in front of the nearest hovel. Below the gardens, they came out into tall grass and crawled on their stomachs. There was a barbed-wire fence around the tomato plants. Renzo reached through it and handed him a tomato. While he was taking the second, a woman came out of the nearest door with a pitcher in her hand. She started toward the road and did not look in their direction. But Renzo started to run and Marcello followed him.

It was when they were climbing back up to the road, near the Trattoria Panorama, that Renzo stepped on a nail.

He was wearing rubber-soled shoes and the nail went into his foot. The next week he did not come to school. A few days after he failed to appear, when Marcello went by his aunt's apartment, the confusion reminded him of the train station the time he and his family had gone to Sicily to visit his grandparents.

Doctors, his aunt and uncle, neighbors from the building, his mother, and a servant were running back and forth. The maid was told to go one place, then as she started she was told to go another. In the confusion, no one prevented him from entering his cousin's room. Renzo was unconscious, but his breath was coming in loud rattles that sounded as though he were talking. Marcello went up to the bed. The shutters of the room were closed and he could not see Renzo as well as he could hear him. There was a short gargle, a long hiss, silence—then it started over again. He waited from one silence to the next, frightened. Then after a gargle the sounds did not begin again. He leaned closer to the bed. There was suddenly another hiss. But it was not like the earlier ones; it seemed to come from farther down in his cousin's body. And the silence that followed it stretched out in a different way from the earlier silences. As he turned to go into the hall to find someone, he met his aunt coming into the room and said to her:

"I don't think Renzo's breathing any longer." He knew of the deaths of relatives and people in the neighborhood, but this was the first time that a friend of his own age had died. And he had been in the room. For the next few days an awe removed him from the sorrow of his relatives. He could not believe that he and Renzo had been together in the field below the tomato garden on Monte Mario and would never be there again. He touched his own body with incredulity. When he was ready for bed, he stood for a minute looking down at his little brother, already asleep in the bed opposite his. Whatever it was that separated them from death was so slight. He felt differently about his father and mother and sisters. He did not know why, but they seemed less threatened. And he realized that he felt awe, and fear, and urgency, but not the sorrow that his relative spoke of as coming from their love.

Perhaps this alone would not have made him question his ability to love. But afterward, when he was faced by his father's feelings toward him and he began to question his own emotions, he was surprised and then frightened to discover the faults that he could see in the people who were close to him. He had been taught manners; he knew not to express unfavorable judgments; but it seemed to him that he should not be able to make these judgments of his father and mother and sisters if what he felt for them was really love.

Was it possible that he was unlike other people? He enjoyed going with his schoolmates to watch a soccer match, or marching half a dozen together to the café at the end of the street near the school and talking while they ate ice cream. But he liked all of them; there was no one who was his particular friend, no one whose absence destroyed the pleasure he took in all the others, as was true for most of the pupils. Among his classmates, he did not even feel the loss of Renzo. He went often in the afternoon to the apartment of Bruno's family, who lived on the floor below his family in the new building. But when he examined his feelings for Bruno, he found that he liked the other members of Bruno's family as much as him, and that it was the added spaciousness and graciousness of the apartment, and playing with the expensive construction toys that Bruno's father bought him, as much as it was being with Bruno, that he enjoyed.

One day after school, when he was standing on Viale Giulio Cesare, looking at the posters outside the cinemas there and pulling his trousers where they were tight in the crotch, he saw a man beside him watching him. When their eyes met the man asked him if he wanted to go inside. He replied that he did not have the money. The man smiled and, touching him, offered to buy him the ticket. He shook his head no. He knew instantly why the man had asked him and he was fascinated, despite his having no intention of complying. The man mistook the meaning of his wide-eyed immobility and said that he would give him some money, too, if he would come. He shook his head again. The man followed him most of the way home. The next day when he told about the encounter to his schoolmates, some of whom he had heard tell of similar adventures, they laughed and said that he was afraid and a monkey not to have gone. Being laughed at displeased him. He did not tell them the next time a similar thing happened. He was inside the same cinema, standing at the back of the auditorium, waiting to see a scene through to the end again before he left, when another man touched him. He moved away and watched until he saw the man go off with another boy. The third time he was at the adjoining cinema with his whole family. It was the first evening they had been out together since his cousin's death. The auditorium was crowded and he was sitting by himself in the row behind his mother and father, his sisters and brother. The man sitting next to him, a shopkeeper or clerk of the neighborhood, as the others had been, touched him as intimately as the first two. He did not move away. And this time, with his family present, when the man indicated that he should follow him to the lounge at the front of the theatre, behind the screen, he went. He did not speak during the occasion. When it was over, the man put several one-hundred-lire coins into his hand. On the way home, he left his family for a moment and hurried by the store where Bruno's father bought him toys and purchased a naval destroyer construction kit that he had had his eyes on. He planned, if he were questioned, to say that Bruno had lent it to him; but no one asked where the toy or the money for it had come from.

After that, it was like magic. Each time, he could not believe that it would happen again. Instead of having pleasure alone, he had it with someone and was given money. The encounters always happened in the cinemas in his neighborhood. After he left them, he did not give another thought to the people whom they occurred with; the money was all that remained. If he ever set out from the apartment with a "happening" in mind, it was more as though he were setting out to dream a certain dream than to encounter anyone. But when he began to ask himself if he were capable of liking, or affection, or love, he wondered if his attitude toward these encounters might not be another example of his callousness.

He reached the steps and ascended slowly, without stopping. The boys who hung out there were not people whom he wanted to know. But he watched, frowning, to see who was present.

By the time he had started to school across the city, he had ceased to go often to the cinemas in his neighborhood. He had outgrown that. Sometimes, when he had had a fight at home, he walked for hours in the far parts of the city and people looked at him the way the men in the cinemas had. But he made no contact with them. Then, one day when he was walking in the Villa Borghese, a man in an automobile drew up and asked him if he wanted to take a ride. The man drove him back to an apartment not far from his own neighborhood. A new type of adventure began. But, although he had gone to apartments a few times, he did not take these encounters as lightly as he had taken the encounters in the cinemas. His awareness was widening, and he had learned that it was best to keep his discoveries to himself, just as it was best to keep his desires from his father. It was by using knowledge, not by talking about it, that he made it his own. To have discussed his adventures with his schoolmates, or to have gone looking for adventures with them, would have violated his growing sense of identity. And there at the Spanish Steps it occurred to him that he was himself because he was the one common element connecting the different spheres of his experience.

When he reached the next-to-last landing, he saw Forrest standing at the balustrade above him. The American was wearing the same beautiful Shetland jacket and cashmere shirt that he had been wearing each of the other times that Marcello had seen him. It was the most interesting thing about this foreigner: the beautiful clothes he owned, as though he cared about them, and the awkward way he wore them, as though he didn't.

Forrest saw him and raised his hand. Marcello waved back and continued up the steps.

The man who had picked him up in the automobile that day in the Villa Borghese had been a Roman, but most of the few people that he had talked to at the Steps were Americans. He imagined them to be very rich and he had been surprised that the first one who had asked him to go home with him had lived in a small room in a pensione and had given him no money at all. He had not asked for any, he would no more ask a stranger for money than, despite his curiosity, he would ask a stranger a personal question. His manners were instinctive. Also, to ask for money would violate his feeling of his own worth. It would demean him in the same way he would be demeaned if he submitted passively to his father's unfair use of his power.

Forrest shook his hand and, introducing him to the man at his side, said that the man was a cinema director.

"Are you an actor?" the man asked.

"I have always thought that I would like to be an actor," Marcello said, wondering why, despite his good looks and his sisters' devotion to cinema stars, the idea had never occurred to him.

A whole new sphere of experience, unconnected to the others, opened before his eyes. He would be able to buy ski pants.

The director, grinning like a clown, talked with Forrest in English and laughed at the end of each sentence.

"What are you laughing at?" Marcello asked.

"Nothing," Forrest said. "At least, I don't know how to explain it in Italian."

Half in gestures, half in words, the director indicated that he had to go somewhere and invited Marcello to join them. They started walking in the direction of the Pincio, beside the wall where he and Forrest had walked the first day.

"He says that you are better-looking than most of the Italian actors," Forrest said, translating one of the director's remarks.

In front of the outdoor café, where workmen were refurbishing the garden behind the ironfence and lining its gravel paths with potted flowers, a group of Italian men rushed up to the director. While the Italians and the director talked, Forrest asked:

"What have you been doing since I saw you?"

To such a general question he could only give a general answer.

"Niente."

The Italians and the director started away; then the latter turned back and, having said something in English to Forrest, added to Marcello with a wink:

"Arrivederci."

"Aren't you going with your friend?" Marcello asked.

"No. What are you doing?"

"Nothing."

"Let's walk."

Forrest did not say where they were walking, but instead of going up toward the Pincio he turned from the dark tunnel of ilexes onto the street that leads down toward Piazza del Popolo, in the direction that Marcello would have to go in any case to catch his bus.

"Who was that man I saw you talking with last week?" Forrest asked. "At the top of the Spanish Steps."

"An acquaintance."

"Italian or American?"

"Italian."

Marcello wondered, as they descended the flight of steps that leads down into the piazza beside the church, if this encounter would end, as that one had, with his merely being walked to his bus stop. On a landing three-quarters down, Forrest stopped to look at a group of kittens who were living behind the open-work iron gate that separated the steps from an odd angle of ground at the side of the church. As he petted them, he said:

"It would please me if you would come back to the house with me. Will you?"

They went directly to the bedroom when they reached the apartment. As Forrest was closing the Persian blinds behind the transparent white curtains, Marcello began to remove his clothes. The bed and chest and chairs in the bare patrician room, so different from the bedrooms in his home where every surface was scattered with clothes and possessions, were as separate and serene as the objects in display windows. Their bareness brought back to him a memory of the pleasure he had experienced there before. Excited, he looked across the room at Forrest, who was undressing and putting his clothes on the other chair. He liked the American's appearance as well as his clothes. He was a large-framed, conventionally handsome man, whose pleasant temper showed in the heavy features of his face, and he had the kind of light brown hair that is so rare in Italians, just beginning to be touched with gray. He, too, seemed separate and serene. On the way to the apartment, he had said that he had a wife and two children, but most of his statements were like the exemplary sentences at the bottom of the pages in a school grammar. In response to an unanswered question, he had said:

"Something extraordinary must have happened to you once to make you so silent."

Now he said:

"Get into bed before you get cold."

He was solicitous, despite his being older, and Marcello wondered if there was someone without any power to whom his father was considerate in the same way.

He caught himself making this reflection. He did not like to compare this part of his life to the other. But he was reassured: no one would know what he had thought. And, looking at Forrest again, he wondered what he was like in America.

"My friend says that the boys in Rome began doing this after the war," Forrest said when they were in bed.

"Your friend is wrong," he replied. "Roman boys have been doing the same thing since ancient times."

That morning he had put on his pink shirt. Later, when he came back into the bedroom to dress, Forrest asked him:

"Did an American give you that shirt?"

"No, I bought it."

"But the writing is in English."

Forrest pointed out the label in the collar: For Men.

"That is the name of a shop here in Rome."

He smiled at the look of incredulity that the American tried to suppress on his face.

"Really, it's true."

"But you know other Americans?"

"No. None."

"Only me?"

"Only you."

His smile was so broad that he could feel the tops of his cheeks pressing against the bottoms of his eyes. The lie made him happy and full of friendliness.

"I must buy me an Italian grammar," Forrest said. "As it is, I'm never sure what I'm saying or what you're saying."

The sound of a door opening and closing reached them from the front of the apartment. Forrest said:

"My friend has come back. He only uses extras in his film. But I will ask him to get you a job if you would like it."

He did not answer.

"Would you?"

He had forgotten this possibility. But being reminded of it made him less able than earlier to expose himself by asking for a favor.

"Yes or no?"

He smiled.

"Answer. I want to hear you speak."

He opened and closed his lips.

"Yes."

The director was standing at a marble-topped table in the front room, mixing a negroni from the bottles of gin, vermouth, and Campari that sat in front of the wall mirror above the table. Forrest accepted his offer of a drink and asked if Marcello wanted one. The idea made him laugh.

"No."

"Why?"

"They are too strong."

"Would you like a glass of wine?"

He shook his head.

"Don't you drink wine?"

"Yes, when I eat."

Forrest offered him coffee. He wanted to be agreeable, but he shook his head again.

"You do drink coffee, don't you?"

"At home in the morning."

The director said that he was sure they could use him. He should write his name and telephone number; they would be given to the Italian casting agent, and the agent would telephone him when he had the schedule of the time and place of the scene that he would be used in.

"It will probably be on a weekday," Forrest said, "when you go to school."

"For this event, I will not go to school."

"Then come into the dining room. There are paper and pencils."

There was also a box of Perugina chocolates, the kind that have liquor centers and are wrapped in gold foil with small bright-colored labels of the products inside, Martell Cognac, Pernod, Bosford Gin.

"Cioccolatini!"

The exclamation escaped him involuntarily, but Forrest looked pleased that something interested him.

"I'd forgotten them. Take one."

He chose a Captain Morgan Jamaica Rum and ate it while he wrote down the information on the pad that Forrest pushed toward him. When he had finished, his eyes passed the candy box.

"Take as many as you like and put them in your pocket."

He selected two.

"One for now," he smiled, "and one for the bus."

As he hurried down the steps, he was glad that he had given more information than had been requested. To make up for his having asked for something, he had included his family's address on Via Giordano Bruno.

CHAPTER 3

One of the confusions of spring, in a climate so nearly ever-green that the trees do not lose their leaves in the autumn, is that the old foliage is shed and the new appears at the same time. Leaves were sailing down from the ilexes and magnolias all around Forrest where he was sitting on a bench in the middle of the Pincio gardens. But when he raised his eyes, the branches above him, instead of being bare, were covered with bright new foliage. Earlier, he had passed a mimosa blooming in yellow splendor at the side of the Spanish Steps. The branches of the leafless Judas trees were pink over the walk below the Belvedere. In the shady flower beds around him, cyclamen and azaleas made patterns of white and lavender.

This confusion of seasons reminded him of his feelings on the day when he had discovered that Marcello lived on Via Giordano Bruno. As he handed the sheet of paper to the director and saw the address, he was overcome with pleasure and regret. He was happy and at the same time anxious that there was something he should do about the coincidence. He wanted to hurry after the boy and bring him back. But when he asked himself what he had not done, or what he could do if Marcello were still present, there was no answer.

The director's attitude had been no help and Forrest had realized that he had been right to hesitate about bringing the boy back to the apartment when the other man would know about it. Behind his cynical façade, the director was promiscuously romantic. He had guessed who Marcello was the day they had seen him at the top of the Spanish

Steps with the airplane bag. That evening he had begun to tease Forrest.

"A wild look came on your face when you saw that boy," he said. "You looked as though wild horses couldn't have torn you away."

It was true that the sight of Marcello disappearing with the unknown man had plunged Forrest into a gloom so great that he regretted the time he still had to stay in Rome.

Then, the following day, the director told him that he had encountered the man and had asked him if Marcello had gone home with him. Forrest could not imagine having such a conversation with a stranger, but the director acted as though it were perfectly natural. The man was an Italian, he said, but not a Roman. He was from somewhere in the north, visiting the city to see his ill sister, and he had told the director that he had not taken the boy home, only walked to the bus with him.

"Maybe he couldn't take him to his sister's house," the director said. "Or, maybe, being an Italian, he *knew* not to trust him."

Forrest, when he found that there was an equivocal explanation of Marcello's going off with the man, felt as though he were freed of the suspicion of a crime. It was clear why Marcello had been talking to the man, no matter what had happened, but he did not want to accept that the boy went off indifferently with anyone who wanted him, although that was what he had done with him. He preferred to shut his eyes to appearances and to leave himself free to accept any other version of events that he could find.

The director's reaction to seeing Marcello's telephone number and address was in keeping with the rest of his attitude.

"Now that you know where he lives, he won't rob you," he said. "But, of course, that won't make any difference if he wants to blackmail you."

Forrest was annoyed with this harping on the criminal. That evening, the director had a group of his co-workers to the apartment for drinks. They struck Forrest as affected and tedious. He could not answer the remarks they addressed to him, and when they were getting ready to go out to dinner, he said that he had an appointment. After the intimacy of the afternoon, he felt more alone than ever. But if he stayed and listened to the director's remarks they would quarrel. And he did not want to quarrel. He wanted Marcello to get his job.

The scene for which Marcello was called was made at night on Via Veneto. It was the last location setting of the film and had been saved to the end because it required a large crowd. Forrest went along and worked as an extra. He hoped that the experience would be interesting, but he was disappointed. The night grew cold soon after the work started. Endless mechanical trouble developed. Shots had to be taken over and the time between shots grew longer and longer. The waiting and doing nothing were worse than in the army. And Marcello did not turn up. Forrest saw the casting agent's list of people who had been called. Marcello's name was among the others. But there was no check by it to indicate that he had reported, and the evening ended without his appearing.

Forrest ignored the director's explanation for Marcello's absence: that he was probably in jail. A few days later, he encountered Marcello in the usual place and was told by him that his father would not let him out of the house at night. He accepted the story for what it was worth. After all, Marcello's story about the man with him the day that he had the airplane bag accorded with the truth as Forrest knew it—not that it was a compromising truth or one that there was any reason to conceal. He was more impressed by the sudden thought that, despite his keeping his eyes open to see him in some unexpected place, he had never encountered Marcello anywhere except at the Spanish Steps. The boy seemed to appear there by magic. Forrest was more often in the blocks around Piazza di Spagna than he was on the Steps themselves. But he had never seen Marcello on a street approaching or leaving, and he had never run into him anywhere else in Rome. He seemed to be a mirage that appeared only in that specific locality. Most strange of all, except for the evening with the airplane bag, he had never seen him already at the Steps waiting, as other people were, but had witnessed his arrival.

Marcello said that he had telephoned the apartment the evening of the film job to explain that he could not come. There had been no one there to answer, but Forrest wondered if the explanation was true. When he had given Marcello the number of the apartment and asked if he would telephone if there was a chance that they could see each other, Marcello had replied with one of the superbly affirmative phrases that Italian is so rich in, "Senz'altro": *yes, certainly, without more ado.* But there had been no call, and Forrest believed that Marcello had wadded up and dropped the paper, just as he himself had wadded up and dropped the page from Robert's notebook the night of Befana.

"I don't believe that you still have it," he said.

"Yes, I do."

"Show it to me."

"I remember it."

Forrest could not give anyone the number without referring to his address book and he was amazed to hear Marcello recite the six digits. The boy shrugged it off.

"I have a good memory," he said. "See, I remembered to bring this."

He reached among the books he was carrying and handed Forrest a schoolchild's Italian grammar.

"Is this for me?"

"Yes."

"Don't you need it?"

"No. There are many at home that no one uses any more. I brought it for you."

"But how did you know that you would see me today?"

"I didn't. But if I hadn't" — an innocent, onesided smile, — "I would have telephoned."

The elements in Marcello's smile were as bewildering to Forrest as the confusion of the seasons. He wanted to reach out and touch the boy's face to convince himself that it was real.

Nevertheless, he did not ask him to the apartment that day. He was having dinner in the evening with a friend of his father-in-law's, an investment counselor with whom he had worked sometimes, and who, it turned out, seemed to have been instructed to find out what was going on with him. The idea of seeing someone who knew his wife and his father-in-law was enough to make him question the sanity of what he was doing. His reason, however, was that he wanted to consolidate this step toward becoming a friend as intensely as any amorous friend can want to consolidate a step toward becoming a lover. The gift of the book was such a simple and friendly gesture, so free of the element that entered when he gave Marcello money, that he did not want the two of them placed side by side. Yet, he thought later, was that not exactly what he did want: for his gifts to be as simple and friendly as the boy's?

They had walked onto the Pincio.

"How often do you go to the Spanish Steps?" he asked.

Marcello gave a long, slowly widening smile, as though to admit that what he was going to say was untrue. But all that he said was:

"From time to time."

"And when did you first start going there?"

Forrest was looking at the side of Marcello's face where the constellation of freckle-flat moles were the same liquid brown as the irises of his eyes. Against his skin, they looked like drops of color, still fresh from the brush of the Maker, left by intention to point out the perfection of the features around them.

Marcello returned his gaze without a flicker and Forrest thought that he was planning his answer. Then he realized that the boy no more intended telling him what he had asked than one of the nearby trees intended taking a step toward him.

They parted without either of them mentioning going to the apartment. Again Marcello agreed to telephone when they could see each other, but another week had passed with no call and no sight of him. He had disappeared, and Forrest pictured him spending his time with the man he had gone down the steps with, anonymously multiplied.

Today, the bench Forrest sat on was not far from where they had been walking. The morning's *Il Messaggero* and a three-day-old copy of the overseas edition of *The New York Times* lay on his lap, unopened. He had said to the news-dealer when he bought them:

"It's spring today."

And the man had replied:

"Yes. It is the twenty-first of March."

A place must be wonderful, Forrest thought, when the people in it consider the miracle of spring so matter-of-factly.

The director had left Rome, but *Il Messaggero* carried forward his picture of a criminal world. At least one corroborating story was in each edition. Italians regularly went with other Italians to their rooms, confiscated their identity papers, and demanded money for their return. An American soldier accompanied a boy to the bank of the Tiber and was beaten over the head with an umbrella. Two adolescent youths murdered a night watchman. One was caught the next day. He had an innocent face, and the story that he told was childishly credible. He and a group of boys in his neighborhood near Ponte Milvio were friends. They shared the common trait, as the newspaper phrased it, that none of them was reluctant, for spending money, to offer himself to the weakness of certain well-known deviates. But their immorality was incidental. Their real interest lay in living an adventurous outdoor life based on incidents that they saw in Western films. They organized searches in the hills outside Rome for buried treasure. Recently, they had decided to live in a grotto near their neighborhood, staying there both day and night. They ate when and how they could, and on the night of the crime their hunger had become so acute that they had gone to a nearby villa and climbed over the wall to steal six goldfish from the pond in the garden and take them back to the grotto to roast over the campfire. When the night watchman surprised them and gave chase, they were terrified. One turned on the guard and shot him. The boy who was caught denied having fired the shot or having had any idea that his missing friend was carrying a gun. Despite the unlikeliness of this last claim, the police seemed to accept the rest of the story. But day after day, as Forrest followed the account in the newspaper, it became apparent that instead of adventurous children the gang were blackmailers and murderers. They had cold-heartedly robbed and killed an aged tobacconist a few weeks before. As the rest of the gang was rounded up, they all looked as innocent as the first one. The ringleader was Sicilian.

Forrest wondered if he was wrong not to connect these stories with Marcello. They were the only source of information he had for the invisible world that the boy had disappeared into. On the other hand, he knew that a conception of the life in New York gathered from the *Daily News* would consist largely of murders, robberies, and traffic deaths. Also, the visible world that Marcello had disappeared into contradicted this version.

The evening that Forrest had gone away on his own from the director and his friends, he had remembered that it was Monte Mario, and not the part of Rome he knew, that Marcello lived in. In Piazzale Flaminio, he caught sight by chance of the number 99 bus that he had taken the night he went to dinner near Piazzale delle Medaglie d'Oro and jumped onto it. Once across the river, the bus started up the long dark street with the lighted fountain in the distance that he remembered from before. But his attitude toward the neighborhood was different this time. Via Giordano Bruno must be somewhere near. The wide tree-lined streets and the solid dark blocks of houses on either side appeared to have been laid out on clear fields around the turn of the century; they gave no hint of having been constructed, like the center of Rome, out of grandeur and rubble. The bright commercial stretches and the dark straight blocks of buildings were a concrete expression of the same rich bourgeois spirit that had constructed Manhattan's brownstones; but here the buildings and neighborhood were set in a landscape that, despite his catching sight of a gasoline service station and a florist shop, was as Eden-like as the Villa Borghese and overcast, like that garden, with the lights and shadows of nineteenth-century romanticism. He felt that he had found the soft surface of the body whose veins and bones he had seen laid bare in the neon signs and marble ruins of the center of the city.

After twisting up the dark hill beyond the fountain, the bus arrived as before in a long new square, sloping at a right angle to the road. A double line of pines was down the center, and on one side a glass-fronted restaurant, its name in neon script across the front, that might have been in Miami Beach. He knew that he should eat, but he did not want to enter such a place. He stopped instead in a bar, ordered a Campari soda, a toast, and had them standing at the counter. After an espresso, he started walking back down the long dark slopes of Viale delle Medaglie d'Oro.

The left side of the street was lined with walled villas. He looked at the signs of the streets leading off on the right in the hope of finding the one he wanted. Buses and automobiles went up and down with an oceanlike swish of passing motors. It was quiet, almost as though he were in the country, but he enjoyed this intimacy more than he would have enjoyed the emptiness of a rural night. Lighted rooms behind the branches and balconies made him aware of the quiet sounds of people nearby. Halfway down the effortless descent, with an idea that the place he was looking for might be in the nest of lighted blocks to the right, he cut off in that direction. The street brought him into a bare, unfinished piazza where people like the people who filled the buses and stores in the daytime were sitting before two cafés. He looked at them as he circled the dusty square, reading the names of the streets leading off. He exited into an unpaved downhill block. On each side, new apartment houses and skeletons of buildings under construction rose from muddy excavations. He could see the backs of the older residences on the street he had been on earlier. But there were no through streets and he began to fear that he would be lost, for he did not know this section and the only way he could return on foot was by keeping the bus in sight and following its turns. At last there was a dirt street to the left. He came out again just above the lighted fountain.

Piazzale degli Eroi is ugly when seen on foot; it resembles a traffic circle on the outskirts of an American suburb. The elevated, electric-lighted jets of water are obviously meant to be admired from a distance; and Forrest, thinking there might be a warning about modern Rome in this, watched until a number 99 bus led him out of the large piazza onto the wide, tree-lined avenue. There were people then, girls and groups of soldiers at the bus stops, but the life was still closed off from the streets and he felt an even greater sense of the nearness of a pleasant warmth in the surrounding barracks-like buildings. But he did not find the street that he was looking for.

Via Giordano Bruno was there, on the other side of the avenue, just below the fountain. But it was daytime when, having looked it up on his map, he went back and found it. It was only three blocks long. The buildings along it were the same five-story condominiums as in the rest of the neighborhood. The one Marcello lived in was the newest and most prosperous-looking. A bougainvillaea-flanked walk led to the entrance on one side. Forrest did not go down it and look at the names on the mailboxes as he wanted to. He did not even cross to that side of the street. He watched from beside an oleander tree on the far sidewalk, trying to see in the earth-colored walls and shuttered windows some revealing difference from all the other buildings. But it looked the same, except for its slight air of prosperity.

At the sight of a woman coming out of the building, he hurried on as though he were late for an appointment. He paused only when he had passed through several streets without thinking where he was and had come out onto Via Cola di Rienzo. Walking along at a slower pace, he experienced the pleasure of looking into the windows of a clothing store and seeing the label For Men in the necks of all the shirts and sweaters on display. When he backed away to read the store-front sign, the electric letters above the entrance gave the noun in the single: For Man.

He mentioned this discrepancy the day that Marcello gave him the grammar and they walked by the bench where he was now sitting. But he did not say that he had seen Marcello's house. He wondered what would happen in that house if he were to telephone. Although he hesitated to enter there even in such an immaterial way, he did not know whether he feared that a telephone call would bring embarrassing questions down on Marcello from his respectable family, or that it would bring Marcello and his father down on him, straight out of the director's and the newspaper's criminal world, with threats of blackmail. He could picture the one eventuality as well as the other. The boy who had gone to bed with him that first day had seemed so untouchable that the bare knowledge that he could be touched had left him with no indication of which of these possibilities was the most likely. He could believe that Marcello had not called him because sex played so casual a part in his life that he only thought of it every week or ten days. At the same time, he could believe that Marcello worked so hard at being picked up, had so many parts of Rome in which he wanted to see if there was someone new for him, and so many regular, and perhaps better-paying, customers, that it was only thus infrequently that he could fit Forrest into his schedule. The only thing that put a stop to these speculations was his remembering that he would be a fool to be suspicious and bring down on himself what he suspected.

He tried to think of Giordano Bruno. His permit to use the Vatican Archives had come and that morning he had made his first visit. He had explained to various people, sometimes in Italian, sometimes in English, what he wanted. Bruno had been arrested and locked in Castel Sant'Angelo. Eight years later, he was brought out one morning and burned alive in Campo dei Fiori. During the eight years, he did not retract his works or admit that they were wrong. He maintained that they were in accord with the Church and that the whole difficulty was a misunderstanding. It was this position of Bruno's as a man who is sure he is in agreement with authority, and who will not falsify his declarations to achieve a nominal accord, that interested Forrest. He wanted to know what had gone on those eight years. Had the pope misunderstood Bruno? Had Bruno deceived himself that they were in agreement? If opposition is inherent between two parties, a lifetime may not remove it, but this had begun with the two parties in accord. How had there come between them a difference that was insoluble and yet that they could not pinpoint and confront each other with? And how does a man spend eight years finding new ways to present the same viewpoint, to develop the same argument?

As so often happens in Italy, the situation at the Archives seemed to be the same at the end of his explanation as it had been at the beginning. He did not know any more than that he was to wait and go back in several days. And as he sat in the garden, he was not sure that he would go back at all. He had seen none of Italy south of Rome. It would be much wiser for him to travel to Naples and Sicily, as he had originally planned, and then go across Calabria to Brindisi and take the boat for Greece. His father-in-law's friend with whom he had eaten had said that Corfu was the most interesting place he had been to. That way, he would escape his indecision about Marcello and his adjacent worry that what he was doing was the worst possible thing for his marriage. He had sent his daughters two postcards that morning, one a photograph of bananas made to look like pigs eating out of a sliced-orange trough, the other of a lemon made into a bride, complete with bouquet and veil. He should write his wife today. But if he was going to leave Rome at the end of the month, he should tell her now and give her a new address. And he could no more make up his mind to leave than he could make up his mind about Marcello, or concentrate on Giordano Bruno, or read the newspapers. He ended by simply sitting and watching what was going on around him.

The gardeners had been trimming everything in the park for the last week, starting with the tops of the trees, and had arrived at the papyrus in the fountain of Herod's daughter. Moses, who had been hidden yesterday in the bulrushes, lay in full sight, surrounded by cut stems. A group of sailors stopped and photographed each other in front of the marble figures. Then a woman sat down on the bench opposite and her two children began playing ball on the gravel around the fountain.

The children were the age of the boys Forrest had seen all winter in Rome, wearing short pants halfway to their knees — halfway, that is, from their waists — sometimes with just sweaters above, as though there were no such thing as the cold, and sometimes with overcoats and scarfs, as though there were no such things as their legs. These two sported summer shirts. The older one was carrying a soccer ball. He stationed himself parallel to his mother's bench and kicked the ball toward his little brother at Forrest's side. The younger boy was too slow for the game. The ball went past him nearly every time and the greater part of his playing was spent in running after it along the paths between the flower beds.

His name was Marcello. Soon the air was full of it. "Attenzione, Marcello! Qui, Marcello! Là, Marcello! Aspetta, Marcello!" Forrest watched and listened. The smaller boy, with his dull-sheened black hair and his large eyes, was what his older namesake must have been at that age. "You're not doing it right, Marcello. It's no fun if you don't do it right." Marcello, almost run off his feet, halted and turned down the corners of his mouth in an effort to hold back the tears. Then he walked off, straight across the path of his brother's gaze, back of the tree behind his mother's bench. He stood there, alone, hiding as well as he could in the open space. "Marcello, vieni qua!" his brother called. "Torna, Marcello!" The name, accented on the drawn-out second syllable, had a falling cadence, a note of infinite longing. Then he switched to a diminutive. "Lello, come on. Don't be angry, Lello. We'll do it another way." Grave-faced, the smaller boy came back and the game went on. This scene had as much as anything to do with the decision that Forrest made. He stayed on the Pincio until the white statues began to glow in the twilight. Then it was time for him to telephone the bindery where he had taken the grammar and ask if it was ready. He returned by way of the Spanish Steps to a bar in Piazza di Spagna and called from there, buying two gettoni for the telephone instead of one. At the Perugina candy store on Via Condotti, he purchased a new sack of cioccolatini al liquore. (He had eaten all the others.) Then he stopped in the shop where he bought foreign newspapers and selected a postcard. At the apartment, he Scotch-taped the extra telephone token on the back of the postcard, which showed a view of the fountain he had been sitting by earlier. He did not write his name or any message. If there were a number of people apt to send a similar reminder, that was his misfortune. He addressed the envelope on the typewriter, put the postcard inside, and dropped it into a letter box on his way out to dinner.

CHAPTER 4

Marcello was returning from Ninì's house, where he had stopped on his way home from his morning classes, when Claudia gave him the heavy, oddly balanced envelope. She wanted to know what was in it.

"Open it here so I can see."

"It may be private."

"Come on, Lello!"

"Not with you looking."

Claudia danced around him, but he managed to see the contents of the envelope before she did.

"What does it say?" she demanded when she caught sight of the card.

"Nothing."

"Who sent it to you?"

"I don't know."

"Ninì?"

"No. Another girl."

"Who?"

"You don't know her."

"If you don't tell me, I'll tell Ninì."

"Go ahead."

"No, I won't. But only because she's sick."

"She's up today."

He had seen Ninì as often as his sisters had since the trip to Terminillo. The excursion had not taken place the Sunday she had said — there was no snow, and he went instead to the Lazio-Milan soccer match at the stadium — but the following Saturday. He had the money then, and as often happened when he had money and his sisters wanted to go along, his father paid for him to go and take them with him. There was a party from their neighborhood that included most of the friends who had been with him at the soccer match. During the trip he was one of their group. But things changed after they arrived.

No one skied; they rented sleds and coasted down the hills. Claudia and he had just arrived at the bottom of a slope when an auto-pullman, turning around, backed into Ninì, who had gone down before them. The wheel struck her foot. Claudia ran to the lodge for a doctor; and Marcello, squatting down in the snow, took Ninì's hand. She was smiling, but tears were rolling out of her eyes; the expression on her face made him want to protect her. He held her hand even after the doctor and their friends arrived. And on the return trip he sat beside her in the pullman all the way, telling her about himself and listening to her talk about her life.

"The doctor says that the bone is mended," he told Claudia, "and that she can start back to work this afternoon."

He had to fit his visits to see Ninì carefully into his schedule. He had once been told that the design of Michelangelo's statue of Moses in the church of San Pietro in Vincoli was determined by the shape of the artist's block of marble; similarly, the design of his day was determined by his father's restrictions. Neither he nor his sisters had apartment keys; they were not allowed away from the house for any of the three meals; and they were forbidden to leave again after supper. This left him free on weekdays from the minute his father went to work after breakfast until dinnertime, and from as soon as dinner was over until the hour for supper. Sunday, however, was different. He might have to spend more time with the family, but the pattern was less strict. His father, so definite in other matters, left it up to him and his little brother whether or not they accompanied his mother and sisters to church. And in the afternoons he never knew whether his mother and father would go somewhere and leave their children on their own, which meant that they could have a friend to the apartment if their father knew exactly who it was, or go somewhere if he knew exactly where, or visit his sister — really the greatest freedom of the three.

He first went by the apartment where Nini's family lived on Viale delle Milizie to ask how she was the Sunday after their return from Terminillo. That morning, he said that he was going to stay in bed during church. As soon as the others were gone, he dressed and shaved — as he did twice a week with his father's razor — and hurried out.

The building that her family lived in was older than the one on Via Giordano Bruno. The rooms were larger and the heavy furniture looked as though it had come with the apartment when it was bought. The only other woman in the family besides Nini was her aunt. Her mother had died when she was born; her father had not married again; and her brothers were like uncles, for the youngest one was ten years older than she was. They had been poor before the war; but since the reconstruction they had begun to make money in shovelfuls, like Uncle Scrooge in *Donald Duck,* Nini's favorite comic. They were ironlike in holding on to their gains, and for a long time after their wholesale clothing store began to show a profit they lived exactly as they had when they were poorer. Now, despite the appearance of the apartment, they owned three consecutive steps of their business: the manufacturing workshop, the wholesale store, and a small elegant boutique that the oldest brother was half partner in with the woman he was engaged to marry. All three brothers dressed elegantly. The oldest drove an Alfa Romeo, the middle a Lancia, and the youngest a Giulietta Sprint.

Ninì told him part of this and he saw part of it for himself that Sunday morning. The apartment door was opened by the oldest brother, a dark-featured man dressed in a white shirt with French cuffs. The maid followed him. When Marcello introduced himself and said why he had come, the brother sent her to say that he was there.

"Ninì told us how you and your sisters took care of her," he added.

This lack of a formal thanks was the full expression of his gratitude.

Ninì received him in her room. She was dressed and the bed was made. She sat on it with her left foot in a cast stuck straight out in front of her, the white plaster shining against a cover more in keeping with her appearance than with the apartment. Everything in the room, in fact, looked as though she had selected it. The chest was filled with bottles and a bright-colored collection of felt puppets and dolls. Despite the feminine ornaments, however, the room did not resemble his sisters' room, just as Ninì did not resemble Claudia or Norma. Her skin showed a plumpness and whiteness that was more suggestive of a woman than of a girl, but she herself seemed less a girl than a child. He felt certain that she was more straightforward than his sisters.

"Why aren't you in church?" she asked.

"I told my family that I was going to stay in bed."

"No wonder your father calls you a liar," she said in her low voice. "It's a good thing that I know from the beginning not to believe you."

"You believe that my father calls me a liar."

He was only with her a minute before her other brothers came in to see him. Her aunt was at church. Her father, in pajamas and a bathrobe, stopped him in the hall as he was leaving and asked his name. When he reached the street, he saw the oldest brother driving away from the parking zone in his red Alfa Romeo.

The next two days he thought of Ninì in the apartment with her brothers and father. When he returned to inquire about her on his way back to school after dinner on Tuesday, he took Claudia with him. His visit today was the first since that Sunday that he had made alone.

"Can I have the postcard, Lello?" He put the telephone token in his pocket and gave the postcard to Claudia. He was at the door of his room when he heard his father exclaim in the kitchen:

"Look, she's taking a bath now!"

It was not the woman Marcello sometimes watched undressing in the building across the street that his father was speaking of; it was one of two parakeets in a cage on the terrace above his mother's geraniums. Norma said that a schoolmate had lent them to her.

"How can you tell which is the female?" he asked.

"The male is the one that talks most."

"No, it's the one with the longest tail."

Claudia, who had gone through the hall door onto the terrace, called:

"Look!"

She passed her hand back and forth before the cage. The parakeets, following her movements, turned their heads left and right in unison, resembling spectators at a tennis match in the newsreel.

In his room after dinner, Marcello took the telephone token from his pocket. He did not know who could have sent it if it was not Forrest. He wondered if he wanted to call him. The telephone at the apartment was in the hall. The freedom to use it gave him and his sisters breathing holes through the wall that their father's restrictions erected around them. Claudia or Norma was always first at the telephone if it rang when they were home—just as one of them was always first at the letter box after the postman—and as they could talk without their father's hearing them, unless he happened to be passing, they could make and receive calls without his checking on them.

Marcello had not telephoned Forrest the evening of the film job to say that his father would not let him come. In truth, he had not asked permission to go. His father talked about how boys should earn their own spending money. But when his daughters chattered about being actresses, he expressed his disdain for the people involved in the cinema industry. Even so, if the job had been in the daytime, Marcello had planned to skip school and stay away from the house during dinner hour. Claudia, who had taken the telephone message from the casting agent, had promised to help him cover up. They might have succeeded, too, with a story about his having been detained at school. The money would have been worth the risk. But there was not a chance that he could have gotten away in the evening.

He had not telephoned since the day he gave Forrest the grammar, either. The American had failed to ask him back to the apartment; the questions he had asked had suggested disapproval; and even his repeated requests to call had seemed a way of dismissal.

The postcard excited his curiosity, however. He telephoned while his father was taking a nap.

"Marcello," Forrest said, pronouncing his name for the first time as an Italian would. "I'd decided that you'd never call."

"I had an extra gettone."

"Then you received my postcard?"

"Yes."

"How did you know that it was from me?"

"Who else would it be from?"

Forrest said something in reply that he could not understand, so he interrupted and asked:

"Listen: when can we see each other?"

"Tomorrow?"

"I can't tomorrow. Perhaps this afternoon."

The view of Monte Mario, when he entered the Villa Borghese from the bus stop under Porta Pinciana, rose up directly behind the galoppatoio. It seemed separated from
him only by the riding ring, the sloping bank of grass beyond, and the clusters of pines and magnolias on the Pincio. He felt that when he walked across the field and up the
bank he would arrive at the white tower of the Astronomical Observatory. The illusion interested him, for he knew
that Piazzale Flaminio, the Tiber, the long stretch of Prati,
and the slope of Via Trionfale lay in between. Space seemed
to have contracted the way his time contracted. He was late
for the appointment. He had taken a bus from school, but
he did not hurry now. He had learned that hurrying when
he was late did not make him arrive on time or, seemingly,
any earlier. So, although he took the short cut that the field
offered, he walked with the pace of an athlete who knows
that hurrying hinders his game and has trained himself to
move with deliberate calm.

He wondered if he would be relieved or disappointed
to discover that Forrest had not waited: He had avoided the
Spanish Steps since the Saturday at Terminillo. When he
was telling Ninì about himself on the bus trip, he had been
aware, as he never had before, of having to leave out the
time devoted to his sexual adventures; and this had given
him a feeling that these new encounters, unlike his earlier
ones, might involve him in complications that he would not
want to be involved in. A memory of this feeling, flicker-
ing across his mind during dinner, had sent him to the telephone: he had learned so well to go straight forward at the
initial sign of fear that he was boldest in situations in which
otherwise he would have been most afraid.

He had never telephoned anyone before for such an
appointment. Now that he had made the call, however, it
seemed right to him. The Italian who had picked him up

in the Villa Borghese had found out his number and called him once. They had made an appointment, but he had not kept it. It would be hard to explain to Ninì what there was in common between him and such a Roman businessman. But this would not be true with Forrest. The coincidence of the American's being interested in Giordano Bruno, and what Forrest was like, would make interesting topics of conversation, ones that neither her girl friends nor the other boys in their crowd could duplicate. There was every reason why he should see Forrest and none why he shouldn't: he missed the pleasure, he liked the money, and with an appointment there was no waste of time.

When he crossed the overpass from the Villa Borghese to the Pincio, Forrest was there, sitting at one of the aluminum tables of the café at the end of the Viale dei Bambini. He asked Marcello to sit down and have a drink.

Marcello ordered a Yoga.

"Apricot."

There was no apricot.

"Peach."

There was no peach, either.

"What is there?"

"Pear."

"All right."

Forrest was smiling. Behind him, the horse-chestnut trees were in blossom.

"What have you been doing?"

In order not to answer "niente," Marcello took out his wallet and showed the photograph that Bruno had made of him and Ninì in the snow at Terminillo. Forrest asked where the photograph had been taken. But the scene in the snow did not interest him for long. Nor did the sad-faced Sardinian donkeys who passed, pulling a cartload of children along the gravel walk.

Marcello had finished his drink.

"Those two women sitting down at the other table," he said, "are Americans."

"How do you know?"

"The way they hook their feet back of the legs of their chairs. Italian women never do that."

"Did you know that I was American when you first saw me?"

"Yes."

"How?"

"Your clothes."

"Most of my clothes were bought in England."

"Maybe. But you don't wear them like the English. And your shoes are American."

"I can't tell American shoes from Italian."

"You, no. I, yes."

They had started walking. Forrest asked:

"Are you in a hurry to go home today?"

Marcello made a noncommittal gesture. He wondered why Forrest did not follow up the question with a suggestion that they go to the apartment. He had decided that there could have been reasons why they had not gone the previous time. They had met by chance and Forrest may have had something else to do. But that could not be the case today. Whether he wants to make love, or wants something else that I have not thought of, he decided, I will wait and find out what it is.

"Come over here and I'll show you something."

He led Forrest across the pavement to a bust of a full-faced, long-haired man with a curly mustache and a brand-new nose.

"Bruno. Your Bruno. Not mine."

Forrest laughed. The statue looked more like an opera singer than a philosopher. But it did not divert him any longer than the photograph had.

I wish, Marcello thought, that as in the case of the Yoga, since I cannot make the right guess, I could ask what he wants.

They were going away from the direction of Forrest's apartment. The green light beneath the heavier trees they had reached made it almost dark. Marcello began to despair. Forrest looked as though he were trying to make up his mind to say something. But when he finally spoke, he asked:

"Who does the cooking at your house?"

He is crazy, Marcello thought. But he answered the question as though it had some meaning.

"My mother."

"Does she do the cleaning, too?"

"Yes, that too."

The two women from the café passed, talking in loud voices.

"You're right," Forrest said. "They are Americans."

They had walked all the way through the Giardino del Lago. As they came out onto a street, Forrest said:

"Today is the day the maid comes to clean my apartment. But she must be ready to leave by now. Shall we go and see?"

On their arrival, the maid was in the front room with her long-handled, polychrome feather duster, making stabs at the tops of the high pieces of furniture.

Forrest sat on the sofa between the tall, white-draped windows and watched her while he caught his breath. When she had finished and gone to the back of the apartment, Marcello assumed his waiting, uninvolved air of someone come to do a service. But Forrest was becoming more accustomed to this confusing alternation of friendliness and shyness.

They were sitting side by side, looking out into the room. This seemed to Forrest the time for him to say what he wanted to say. But Marcello could not get comfortable on the sofa. He was equally ill at ease lying back against the cushions, sitting upright, or leaning forward. And now that they were in the apartment, he kept his eyes lowered to his lap or to a spot in front of him on the floor, as he had the first day.

Forrest did not think that the maid's presence had depressed Marcello, but the boy smiled every now and then and when he smiled the change was so enormous that he looked desolate in between.

"Soon," Forrest said, "I must tell my landlady whether or not I am going to renew my lease here at the end of the month."

"Which will you do?"

A question about himself was more encouragement than Forrest usually received.

"I don't know. I want to stay. But I am here alone now and if I stay I want to see you more often."

Marcello nodded.

"Don't say that I can unless you mean it."

"Yes. Senz'altro."

Forrest decided not to mention the results of his previous *senz'altro*.

"Do you know why I sent you the postcard?"

"Because you wanted to see me."

"Yes, but do you know why I wanted to see you?"

One of Marcello's smallest smiles was his answer.

"Yes, I know. But I want to say something else. When I first came to Rome—"

A larger smile accompanied the correction that Marcello made of the auxiliary of *come*.

Forrest's heart sank. After the correction, he could not

say what he had wanted to say. His words were too emotional to submit to this clear-eyed reception just because time was available. He had wanted to say: When I first came to Rome, everything was familiar and unreal. You were the first thing that was different. What I am asking you is to make Rome, and everything else, real again.

Instead, he said:

"When I first came to Rome, I forgot all the words that I looked up in the dictionary. But I never forget a word that I learn from you."

"You forget *sono venuto* and *sono andato*."

"Yes, but I learned those wrong before."

Touching Marcello's forehead, eyes, ears, nose, mouth, lips, and chin, he said:

"Fronte, occhi, orecchi, naso, bocca, labbra, mento."

The closed-lips smile that greeted his words made him add:

"And senz'altro."

"I have a trigonometry test on Monday," Marcello said. "But after Monday I will not have to study so much and I will come to see you when you like."

Forrest had accomplished what he had wanted to accomplish, and so quickly that he did not know where to go from there. Marcello, with such a victory, he was sure, would not for a moment be at a loss for what to do. But his joy made him aware, with a thrill of contrariness, that it would have been much better for him if he had failed and left Rome. He suddenly longed for the small, sure, bed-sized plot that he had formerly had. Nevertheless, having made this gain he was determined not to go back to the game of questions and answers.

"Perhaps sometimes," he said, "I can read Italian to you and you will correct my pronunciation."

"Yes. Now if you wish."

Forrest fetched an Italian book and began to stammer out the words. But his mind was not on them. It was a mistake to read when they wanted to do something else. They were like two people in a train station, both waiting as Marcello had been waiting the first day. Any minute, he feared, Marcello might despair of the maid's leaving and say that he must go.

At a bang from the back of the apartment, Forrest closed the book,

"I think that she's finished. I'll go and see."

The noise had sounded as though the maid were putting away the ironing board. But when he reached the back, he saw to his dismay that she was setting it up.

"I thought that you were finished."

"No, there is still the ironing."

He looked with impatience at the large pile of laundry.

"I must go out soon. Iron only the shirts and leave the rest for next time."

When he returned to the front room, he took the cioccolatini from the table beneath the wall mirror and offered them to Marcello. The grammar, back from the binders, was on the table beside the candy. As he sat on the couch again, he turned over in his mind the idea of asking Marcello to write in the book. The request was unguarded, but it was not as unguarded as what he had been intending to say. And he was having luck. They had already been together longer than ever before.

"I don't think she'll be much more time."

Marcello still might leave before the maid did, but it was clear that he did not want to.

"Once," Forrest said, "I knew a young man who worked for a large company that sent him around the United States inspecting their factories. When he reached Chicago, he married a woman twice his age. His family had the marriage annulled and brought him home. For three years, he worked in the same city without leaving it. Then the company sent him around the United States again, and when he reached Chicago he married the same woman."

The maid was in the entrance hall, changing her shoes. Forrest gave Marcello a fountain pen and told him that he would like him to write something in the grammar.

Earlier, when they had been sitting on the sofa, Forrest had said:

"You are only at ease with me lying down."

It seemed true. As soon as they were in bed, Marcello's distance, awkwardness, and waiting vanished. His childish eyes, which had sought the floor or had looked into a no-where just above their lowered lids — with a reflective quality that made it impossible for Forrest not to feel that the mind behind them was full of unspoken thoughts — sought him as directly as the hands and lips. To his comment on the sofa, Marcello had slyly replied:

"We talk better in the other room."

And Forrest had to admit:

"Yes, we talk better in here."

It was true, literally. When he spoke in the intimacy of their physical touching, in the closeness of their two faces, with all Marcello's impassivity and silence concentrated in the accepting depths of his eyes, the words he spoke no longer had the effect of artifice and recitation. They seemed to proceed naturally from the situation; to be accepted, as he was accepted; and to reach their goal, whatever effect they might have there.

Their effect was not always what was intended. Forrest wanted to say that the next Saturday was his birthday. Marcello replied:

"Yes, it is her birthday. How did you know?"

"Her birthday? Whose birthday?"

"Ninì's. The girl in the photograph."

"I am not talking of Ninì. I said that it is my birthday. Saturday."

"Then you were born on the same day. Saturday is her birthday, too."

This coincidence, on top of the one of Giordano Bruno, just seemed to Forrest to carry on the naturally extraordinary order of things.

"Anyway, that is not what I want to talk about," he said. "We will start over again. I would like to give you a present. But I do not want to choose it. A present that you do not want is all right from someone you love. The person lends value to the present. But with other people the present has to lend value to the person. So, if I am to give you something, it must be something that you want."

This was difficult for him to word in Italian, but the idea got across.

"What would you like?"

"I don't know."

Forrest interpreted this to mean: I don't know if I should say.

"Say."

The decision was slow in arriving.

"A shirt, perhaps."

"Very well. Look, and when you see a shirt that you like, tell me the store and I will buy it."

"Can't we look together?"

"When?"

"Now?"

Marcello opened the grammar as they were leaving the apartment and held it out for Forrest's approval of what he had written.

A Forrest
con simpatia
Marcello

The heaven and earth are mixed up in Italy, and never more than at twilight. It was seven-thirty, the busiest time of the Roman shopping day. The swarms of people in the streets repeated the swarms of swallows over the rooftops, and the neons of certain signs were the pink of the sunset and the blue of the evening star.

At a corner, as they were waiting for the traffic to pass, Forrest wondered it Marcello did not mind being seen in the crowd with him. Surely there might be some of Marcello's relatives or schoolmates among the people jostling each other over every inch of the uneven cobblestones. He himself felt a little obvious.

But, he thought, if I had accepted the young theological student that the cardinal offered to find for me, might not we be going about in the same way? And perhaps there is a similar rationalization that makes it all right for him.

In any case, Marcello's apparent ease inspired him to hazard one more question.

"Do you have other friends that you see often?"

"Yes—" Marcello smiled, as though he were waiting for the noise of a tram to pass. " —school friends."

Despite his tentativeness in saying what he wanted, there was nothing in the least vague about the kind of shirt that he wished to have. It had to be a sport shirt, either Lacoste or Fred Perry, solid in color, with a narrow darker stripe along the edges of the collar and the short sleeves. He explained this to the clerk in the first store they went to. When a shirt was produced that fulfilled all the specifications except the last, he quietly rejected it. The second store had the shirt but in the wrong size. He succeeded at the third. The color was not quite the shade that he wished, but near enough.

Forrest had not given him the usual money when they were at the apartment. Part of his desire to give a present had come from his wish to escape the commercial basis they were on. But as they were walking toward the crowded bus stop where they would part, he got cold feet. He had not said that the shirt was instead of the money and he knew that he could get by without mentioning it now. But he was not sure that he wanted to. His wish, had been to give something besides what the boy expected, not merely to substitute an object for cash. The object was more valuable. But what if Marcello had come to see him wanting the usual sum for a specific purpose? His pleasure in receiving the shirt would be canceled by his disappointment in not getting the money. He might look for the money somewhere else.

"I forgot the money," he said. "Do you want it now?"

For an answer, he received the smile that came nearest to an articulated yes. He reached into his pocket.

"What do you do with this money?"

The smile, as he now knew that it was capable, opened out into words.

"I am always buying things."

"What things? Cioccolatini?"

Not only words but laughter escaped from the upturned lips.

"No, not cioccolatini."

"What?"

A shrug-smile.

"Things."

The inscription in the grammar, when Forrest first saw it, made him aware that there might be a hint of irony in the word *simpatia*. The trouble in understanding a language not your own is that you can never be sure that the syllables mean to you what they mean to the native who uses them. He had not lingered on the thought; while he was with Marcello he was too pleased to be upset, and he had concentrated on enjoying their added time together. But when he returned to the apartment alone the idea came back to him.

Delighted to have something specific to do, he took his Italian-English dictionary and sat down at the dining room table to see if he could pinpoint the shading of the word. The translation for *simpatia* was the trio *liking, sympathy, weakness.* He turned the book cautiously to the English section. No, *pity* was *pietà. Sympathy* was *compassione. Weakness* was *debolezza.* Hopefully, he looked up *friendship.* The only translation was the word he knew, *amicizia.* More hopefully, he looked up *fondness,* but that was *affettuosità indulgente. Liking* was what he was left with: *gusto, inclinazione, simpatia.*

That evening at the trattoria he asked the son who worked as a waiter:

"What is the exact meaning of the word *simpatia?*"

The boy looked serious, as though he were computing a bill.

"It is not exactly *amore.*"

"*Amicizia?*" Forrest offered.

A smile.

"No, it is more than *amicizia.*"

"Is it nearer to *amicizia* or *amore?*"

"Oh, to *amore.*"

"Truthfully?"

"Oh, yes, much nearer to *amore.*"

Both of them were laughing.

"You are happy?"

"Yes, yes."

CHAPTER 5

Other things than sex were like magic to Marcello and difficult for him to believe when they recurred.

One was a dream that surprised him each time that he dreamed it just as much as it had the first time.

In the dream he found money, not a single coin or bill but a vein of coins and bills. The money was lying in the dirt of an unpaved street in his neighborhood. He was walking near the curbstone when he saw a fifty-lire piece, half covered by dust, and picked it up. As soon as the first coin was in his hand, he saw another that the taking of the first had partly uncovered. He picked up fifty-lire pieces, hundred-lire pieces, and five-hundred-lire bills. He did it in a hurry, afraid that someone might arrive and begin to take the others. But he could never get all of them. A new one always appeared, lying loose in the dirt a little way farther on, uncovered by the one that he had thought was the last. He woke up breathless, hardly able to believe that the money was not real, just as he hardly had been able to believe that it was real those first days in the cinema on Viale Giulio Cesare.

His relations with Forrest and Ninì developed a quality that was very much like that of the dream. He saw Forrest more often than before and, besides the presents, was given the same amount of money each time. Then Ninì, too, began to give him presents. When she first was well enough to go out after her accident, he had been content to see her among their crowd. And when she began to want to see him away from the others, he was particularly pleased because he became to them "Ninì's friend." But there was something more in her liking of him than he had counted on. If she had told him right off what it was, he might not have been so interested. But she had made him curious. He wanted to know what he was not told — the same way that he liked to tell what he was not asked — and she resisted all his demands for a reason the day she gave him her first present, an English regimental striped cravat.

He had given her a present first, it was true: a pair of curved enamel cuff links on her birthday, a couple of weeks before. But that was no reason.

"Why are you giving me a present?"

"I don't know. I just remembered that you like this kind of cravat."

"Do you think it's my birthday?"

"No."

"But what made you think of it?"

"The colors, perhaps. They look good on you."

The strangest thing was that the day she gave him the cravat he had come from seeing Forrest, who had given him a summer belt in the same shades of blue and yellow. Forrest had selected and bought the cloth-and-leather belt and presented it to him as he was dressing to leave. When he tried the belt on it was too large. Forrest said that it had come from The Sportsman on Via Condotti and that he would change it. Or Marcello could change it.

Marcello, remembering the pleasure Forrest had seemed to have shopping with him for the shirt, suggested: "Why don't we go together?"

They walked to the store and he changed the belt for a smaller size. Then, when he met Ninì at the Las Vegas Bar on Via Premuda, she gave him the blue and yellow cravat. They had made the appointment the day before. She had told him that she was taking something from her brothers' store to the workshop the next afternoon and that she would slip away afterward and meet him at the café where he and his friends gathered. He already had the appointment with Forrest, but it suited him to meet her just after he had seen Forrest. The money made him able to pay for something if he wanted to, and the calm from which he reassured himself that what he had done a short while before was not important enabled him to flirt with her much more forwardly than he would otherwise have dared.

The only trouble was that he could not always judge how long he would be with Forrest. Often, as on the afternoon when they had changed the belt, he was late.

"You were supposed to be here twenty minutes ago," Nini said.

"I know. I'm sorry. Does the cravat come from your brothers' store?"

"No. I saw it in the window of another shop."

He had told Nini about Forrest. As he had imagined, it was more interesting that way. His acquaintance with Forrest accounted for how he spent some of his time and made good conversation. He had met the foreigner, he said, with one of his schoolmates at the Spanish Steps. He described Forrest's beautiful clothes and the American way he wore them, his oddly pronounced Italian and the childish mistakes he made in grammar. But Forrest was molto simpatico, he added; very appreciative of the help he was given in pronunciation and in finding the things that he wanted to see in Rome.

Nevertheless, he did not admit that he had come from seeing Forrest on the occasions when he met Nini, and he never used his having seen Forrest as an excuse for his being late. Instead, he shifted around the order of the things he had done. The afternoon that Nini gave him the cravat, he said that he had just come from the errand that he had run for his father before school. To back up his lie, he pointed out that, being watchless, he found it difficult to know the exact hour. The result was that on the Sunday after her brother's wedding she gave him a wrist watch.

The wedding was elegant. It did not take place at San Giuseppe in their neighborhood, but at the Church of Santa Sabina on the Aventine. Bouquets of flowers lay on the marble floor for the length of the church on either side of the aisle; Ninì and the other bridal attendants were dressed alike, carrying bouquets of similar flowers. The occasion was important for her; she had made the particular point that Marcello should be her escort and that the whole family should meet him and know that she liked him. He went with her afterward to the reception.

They were walking in the Villa Borghese the next day when she gave him the watch. He had decided that it might be interesting to introduce Forrest and Ninì, and the Villa Borghese was the place where they would be most apt to meet. His mood was optimistic. The grades he had made on his school tests, not just in trigonometry but in the other subjects, had all been passing. His father had not lost his temper with him that day at dinner. And he and his sisters were on particularly good terms. He had left the house with Claudia and Norma, who could not have come out alone without him. Then Claudia and Norma had gone and picked up Ninì, who could not have come out alone with him. The four of them had met Norma's fidanzato and a girl who went to school with Claudia and taken the bus to the Villa Borghese. They were to meet later at Porta Pinciana to go back together.

He had noticed that Ninì was carrying her pocketbook, a thing she did not usually do, but had decided that it was because it was Sunday. She was wearing a plain skirt and an open jacket, with a white shirtwaist and the cuff links that he had given her in the sleeves. The shirtwaist showed off the fullness of her breasts and made her look more mature than ever. She kept smiling, as though she had a secret. She would not tell him what it was. Then, when they were alone, she opened her pocketbook and took out the package.

He opened it tentatively, but he exclaimed with delight when he saw what it contained.

"So that you won't always be late," Ninì explained.

"But it looks expensive."

"Not too much. I bought it from a friend of my brothers'."

They were near the entrance of the Giardino del Lago. In front of the gate, a cluster of many-colored balloons, some with rabbit ears, were moored by long strings to a net of heavier rubber balls on the gravel walk. The balloons rose high enough to catch the wind, as well as the sun, and they pulled the netful of balls along the gravel as though they wanted to escape.

"I'll buy you a balloon," he said. "Which kind would you like?"

"One with rabbit ears. I remember your making rabbit ears on your head with your hands that night at the dance."

"I didn't know that you were interested in me then."

"I was."

"Why didn't you tell me the day when we rode back from Terminillo?"

"We were talking about other things."

The park was full of people, but he steered her along the path beside the galoppatoio where there were mainly couples interested in each other.

"Do you know what my brother's wife told me yesterday? She told me that you are very handsome."

He kissed her. It was not the first time, but it was the first time that he slipped his tongue between her lips. She held onto him more firmly than he did onto her.

"When you are graduated from school," she said, "I hope that you won't leave Rome and go on a ship."

"I won't be graduated for two more years."

"I know. But that's what I hope."

"I hope what I told you the other day."

"What?"

"That I can get a job after school is out for the summer and not have to work for my father."

"Did you have a fight with him today?"

"No. But there's always a chance on Sunday."

"Listen. Next Sunday my brother and his wife won't be back from their honeymoon and everyone else is going to be away from the house, even my aunt. My father may be there, but I can always get away from him. Let's go to Ostia. Just the two of us. It'll be the first swim of the summer. Please."

They had stopped walking. He was leaning back against a wooden fence rail, holding her in front of him, between his legs, as he had often seen older boys holding girls. He half wished that he had been that day, too, to see Forrest before he came to see her. He was excited, and he did not want to become too excited. But he pulled her against him.

"Agreed. We'll go."

"And the watch will help you to be on time."

Despite the watch, they were late joining the others and had to run to catch the bus. Now that they were at ease with each other, they did not stand on the platform at the back but pushed forward for seats. When they were sitting down, it was with the same magical ease of other recent events that Norma's fidanzato leaned forward from the seat behind Marcello and said:

"Where I work, they need boys for jobs this summer, if you're interested."

Norma's fidanzato lived in their neighborhood. She had met him at church and he had given her the parakeets which she had told her parents were lent to her by a girl friend. She was already fond of him and had introduced him to her father and mother when he took a job working as an assistant in a beauty parlor. Now, she was afraid of what her father would say when he discovered that the person she liked was working in that profession. His job was in a branch shop off Piazza di Spagna. They hired extra help for the tourist season, he said, and he was sure that if the manager liked Marcello he could have a job in one shop or another.

Marcello and his sisters laughed all the way up Viale delle Milizie about what their father would think if he had such a job. Norma's fidanzato promised to telephone during the week and let Marcello know when he could introduce him. The last thing Ninì did when they left her in front of her house was to whisper in his ear to remember about Ostia.

Monday, Marcello bought a new black bathing slip in a shop on Via Cola di Rienzo. After he had paid for it he did not have money left for the trip on Sunday. But he was sure to see Forrest during the week. He was not worried.

He telephoned Forrest on Thursday. There was no answer. He called again three times on Friday. That night, Norma's fidanzato telephoned and said that he had arranged to introduce Marcello to the manager on Saturday. He should meet him outside the shop where he worked at eight o'clock, wearing a jacket and a shirt with a tie, and they would go to the nearby hotel where the manager had his office. Marcello wished that the appointment was in the daytime so he could keep it without his father's knowing, but he was so worried by the knowledge that he would have no money for Sunday that he did not mention it.

He telephoned Forrest again on Saturday morning. No answer. Forrest, he decided, must have left Rome for several days and when he returned it would be too late. Feeling too depressed to go out, he spent the morning at home. Everyone else was happy. His little brother and a group of his friends were shouting and chasing each other on the terrace. His sisters and some of their schoolmates were in their room, gossiping and playing phonograph records. Every now and then one of the girls came out and asked him some absolutely pointless question. He wandered from his room to the front of the apartment and back. His mother was cooking. She had prepared polpo alla luciana for him and his father and she was making a dish of boiled potatoes and artichokes for his sisters and Franco, who would not eat seafood. Each time she encountered him, she looked surprised. Well, when he wanted her to have his good clothes ready for him to go to see about the job in the evening, she would not be able to say that he was out of the apartment all the time.

At noon, he lifted the telephone and dialed Forrest's number once more. He no longer hoped to find anyone at the apartment. He did it just because he had gotten used to calling, and he was taken by surprise when Forrest answered. Forgetting what he wanted, he said simply:

"I telephoned you three times yesterday."

He did not ask if they could see each other; Forrest asked the question for him, and when he agreed, asked the hour.

"Four-thirty or five."

By then his father would have gone back to work, and it would leave him plenty of time to see Forrest and come back to the house before he went to meet Norma's fidanzato.

At dinner, even his father was cheerful. He had been contacted by one of Signor Tocci's old customers that morning. No deal had gone through, but if one did it would mean supplying tiles for a whole new group of buildings. This was the kind of contract that brought in real money. The rest of the family, glad to have him in a good humor, acted as though he already had the money in his hands. As he was rising from the table, he said to Marcello:

"I want you to help me on the truck this afternoon. Be ready to leave with me when I go."

Marcello opened his mouth, but it was too late. His father had left the room without waiting for him to reply.

"Mamma, I have an appointment with some friends this afternoon."

"You'll have to break it."

"Why should I break it when he doesn't tell me until the last moment?"

"Well, your father doesn't ask you to help him often. And he has been fairly generous with you lately."

His father had given him nothing the last few times that Marcello had worked for him. But he knew that his mother was referring to his new clothes and the impossibility of telling her the truth angered him.

"I'd rather get a job and work and never take his money."

"All right," his mother replied evenly. "But until you have a job and aren't taking his money, do as he says."

She removed his empty plate and started away.

"How can I get a job if I'm not allowed to look for one?"

"Who doesn't allow you?"

"That's what my appointment is for this afternoon."

"You said that it was with friends."

"It is. But one of them is going to introduce me to the manager of a shop who wants to hire someone for the summer."

"At what time?"

He stared at the tablecloth, looking as unhappy as possible.

"Around seven."

"You'll be finished by then. If not, explain to your father and ask him to let you leave a little early."

"But I am supposed to help my friend do something first."

"He'll understand. He has a father."

"Besides, I have to change into my suit before I go to see the shop manager. There won't be time."

Franco ran in from the terrace.

"The parakeets have laid an egg!"

"How do you know?" Marcello demanded.

"I saw it."

"You've been poking at them with that stick again."

"No, I haven't."

"Yes, you have."

"Lello, leave your little brother alone."

After he had looked at the egg, which was really there at the bottom of the nest in the parakeets' cage, he lay on the bed in his room, rehearsing the words with which he would refuse to accompany his father. But when his father called to him through the door to get ready, he rose and changed his clothes. He wore an old dirty pair of white khaki wash trousers and defiantly drew his new belt through the loops. Then he put on a short-sleeved silk shirt with vertical stripes that had been his favorite the summer before. It was too threadbare to wear when he was going to see anyone, but it was a shame to wear it to do this. He let it hang down over the belt.

The worst thing about working for his father was that it consisted largely of standing around and doing nothing. He was aware all the time of what a waste it was and that he might as well be somewhere else doing what he wanted.

First, he waited at his father's kiln. Then he waited at the garage. At a quarter of six they were still waiting at the customs office behind Stazione Termini for his father to sign the papers for the crates they were to pick up.

There were two workers from the kiln with them and it seemed to him that they could do what they were doing as well without him. Finally, all the formalities were finished and his father came out. It took only a few minutes to load the truck. His father tested the crates, then tested them a second time. They were ready. Tentatively, he said:

"Papa, I've an appointment this afternoon. Will we be finished before seven?"

"Yes, we're finished here now."

Encouraged, he got into the truck. But as they started off, his father, in a knelling tone of final disillusionment, told the driver to stop on Via del Tritone where they had to pick up something from a store. Until then, Marcello had hoped that if he asked to be let out on the way back to the kiln he might be free in time to see Forrest. Now his hope vanished.

It was unfair. Forrest would be disillusioned in him. He would not have the money to go to the beach with Ninì and would have to make up some story. As likely as not, something would go wrong with the appointment for the job this evening.

At Via del Tritone, he got down from the truck and started into the store with the others. His father stopped him.

"Wait with me," he said. "There's only one piece. They can carry it."

His hope revived. They were only a few blocks from Forrest's apartment. He could be there in two minutes. It was worth making the effort. He waited, so his father would not know that he was anxious. Then he asked casually:

"If you don't need me here, can I go now, Papa?"

"Why?"

"The friend I have an appointment with works near here. I just want to tell him that I may be a little late."

"How long will it take?"

Should he say a short or a long time?

"Five minutes."

"Very well."

"Thanks, Papa."

As he started, his father added:

"But be at the kiln by the time the truck gets there, or you won't be able to leave by seven."

He rushed on, refusing to show his disappointment. His effort had failed. But he must pretend to go where he had asked permission to go. Then, as he reached the other side of the street, a new hope rose. There would be at least a minute to see Forrest and explain why he had not come when he had said that he would.

Running, he felt the heat for the first time that year, like a sudden hallucination of summer. In the glaring light, there passed the shop where Norma's fidanzato worked. On one of the white stripes of the pedestrian "zebra" on the street in front of it, he saw a white poodle sitting, presumably safe, but invisible.

The four flights to the apartment left him winded. He was panting when Forrest opened the door.

He smiled and slipped inside. Still in the entrance hall, he told what had happened to detain him. Then, aware of the expectation in Forrest's happiness, he added quickly:

"And I can only stay two minutes."

He wanted a glass of water. The telephone rang while he was asking for it, and he went back to the kitchen to get it himself.

When he returned, Forrest, hanging up the telephone, said:

"That's a beautiful shirt."

He looked down at the shirt with surprise and lifted it to show that he was wearing the belt. Then he hiccuped.

"You drank the water too fast," Forrest said. "Sit down and be calm for a minute."

He sat beside Forrest on the sofa, pleased that he had come but suddenly unsure why he had come.

"Can you come back later?"

"No, I have to help unload things at the kiln and then go home."

"What about tomorrow?"

Remembering the money, he dropped his eyes to the flowers of the sofa upholstering.

"Tomorrow I want to go to the beach with my girl friend. If I can."

"Can't you?"

"I don't have the money."

Forrest laughed.

"Would you like me to give it to you?"

He looked up. As before, the word would not come. But he nodded.

"If possible."

Forrest drew a thousand-lire note from his pocket.

"Is this enough?"

Pleasure overcame his embarrassment and widened in a grin.

As he sat there, his smile crinkling his eyes, unable to say thank you, Forrest reached out and pushed his hair down into his eyes with an affectionate gesture. It was time for him to leave, but he remained sitting on the sofa, thinking that he should get a haircut and wishing that he had not caused Forrest a disappointment as great as his own disappointment had been a short while earlier.

"I can come and see you Monday."

"Monday afternoon is when the maid comes. Remember?"

"I can come in the morning. I don't have to go to school. And my father never wants me in the morning. But you go out then."

"For this event," Forrest said, "I will not go out."

A black storm cloud covered the sky, darkening the room. Marcello rose and walked to the window.

"If it rains tomorrow," Forrest asked, following him, "will you telephone me?"

"Yes."

Forrest laughed. There was a low rumble of thunder.

"I hope that it rains."

"I don't think that it will," Marcello said. "I think that tomorrow will be a clear day."

At the door he kissed Forrest. Then he ran down the steps and all the way to the bus stop at Porto di Ripetta.

CHAPTER 6

Flights of swallows filled the sky after Marcello left. Squeaking swoops of them, flying low over the tile rooftops, remained in the starting rain. They disappeared only at the blackest moment, after the downpour turned to bouncing hail.

Forrest, pleased and disappointed, stood at the window, thinking of Marcello's affectionate gesture and hoping that he had reached where he was going before the cloudburst. Then he picked up the newspaper that he had been reading before Marcello arrived and looked again at the horoscopes for the day.

In the last weeks, since Marcello had begun to telephone, Forrest had read the horoscopes regularly. His life was conditioned to such a great extent by circumstances as far beyond his control as the conjunction of the planets and the houses of heaven that these short sentences seemed as pertinent as anything else. They spoke almost exclusively of money and love, *gli affari* and *amore,* and in a manner that he felt surely must be different from the forecast in non-Mediterranean countries. Good or evil would come from someone young or old, *una persona giovane* or *anziana.* Some forecasts seemed designed for boys like Marcello. "Protection of an older man. The situation will end with movement of money to your use." Others, to bring expectation into situations like his. "Return of a lost person or object. Magnificent romantic opportunity in the late afternoon." The warnings were less clear. "Patience. Even if you change

your mind, think twice before declaring your intentions."
(Which set of intentions?) "To avoid trouble, keep business
and love life strictly separate." (How?)

He did not follow the advice: but concerning Marcello,
whose appearances and absences he knew no reasons for,
he liked to think that the predictions carried some weight, if
only through the possibility that Marcello might read them
and guide his conduct accordingly. He was pleased when
the boy's forecast read: "Good opportunity to profit from a
recent acquaintance." Or: "Your personality alone will not
triumph; make an effort to please those who love you." He
was disappointed by: "Nervous day. The less activity the
better. Stay home and read a good mystery." Enigmatically,
he had liked that morning's "Be faithful."

His own forecast was no help: "Do not give credit to the
dreams of the night or to the fantasies of those around you.
Physical energy necessary in this particular moment."

He walked to the window. The hail had become rain
again, but there was now lashing wind and lightning and
loud claps of thunder. He closed the windows and returned
to one of the upholstered chairs, bringing with him a novel
that he had been reading the night before. On the page
where he had left his marker, he had underlined: "It makes
such a difference when you see a person with beautiful
things behind him unexpectedly."

It was true. In fiction, physical beauty has a hard time
carrying the weight assigned to it. But in life, being with a
beautiful person, surrounded by beautiful landscapes, com-
bines the real and the ideal in a manner that holds the attention as it usually is held only by people and places seen
for the first time He was sure that in any other place than
Rome he would not have entertained the idea of believing
in Marcello's affection for him. Even yesterday, he would
have doubted that such a simple thing as Marcello's appear-

ance in the gaudily striped silk shirt that he had been wearing instead of his usual subdued garments, and his joyous lifting of it to show the belt, could have made so new and pleasant a demand upon his already strained credulity.

In the last weeks, an even more remarkable change had begun. The old Rome that he had known was disappearing and a new Rome was taking its place. All over the city there were sights that drew him out of himself, not through an attraction that he recognized in them, but through an obscure affinity that returned and persisted beyond his understanding. Certain street corners, certain glimpses of park, seemed to have a hidden importance and to hint to him that a time would come when their meaning would be revealed. They were not famous places; they were not places that he had been with Marcello; often, they were not even places that had impressed him when he first saw them. But they kept reasserting themselves in the way that, in his youth, certain books which had meant nothing to him at the time had kept reappearing until he read them. They were real in the way that the trees, the banisters, the backyard dump heap of his childhood had been real; they held no significance that he recognized, but he felt that he would live with them for the rest of his life.

It was this change that had enabled him to return to the Vatican Archives. One morning, as he was walking down the uneven curve of ground between the dark arches of the Theatre of Marcellus and the broken white marble columns of the Temple of Apollo, near Rome's crowded ghetto section, it had occurred to him that all Rome is a backyard. It has the same dump-heap disorder, the same intimacy, of the plot of ground behind a house that catches the objects discarded from it. The children around him, kicking a ball, were as at home beneath the walls of the two-thousand-year-old theatre as his schoolmates had been at home playing baseball in his backyard when he went to school. And he was as at home as they were. Nothing separated him from the weeds, the cobblestones, the monuments. They meant no more to him, but they meant no less, than those rostral columns and bus stops that sometimes made his heart so mysteriously contract. And when he reached the apartment and sat down at the marble-topped table in the dining room, the prison cell in the basement of Castel Sant'Angelo, the fire in the center of Campo dei Fiori, had taken on a reality not unlike that of the oleander-lined street below Piazzale degli Eroi, a reality that he once more felt it worthwhile to investigate and record.

He put down the book and returned to the window. The wind had died down, but the tiles of the roof across the way were still streaming with water. Once, when he had smoked, he had had the frustrating experience of wanting to light a cigarette and discovering that he was already smoking one. The same thing happened to him now; he suddenly longed to be in Rome and was confronted by the fact that he was in Rome. He was homesick for the place where he was. It was a happy homesickness, but he wanted to go somewhere and do something, as strongly as a man who has taken poison may want to go to a pharmacist and buy an antidote. The emotion was so physical that he experienced it only as an impulse to move; he discovered himself crossing the room without knowing where he was going. The rain prevented him from leaving the house, but his experience had been the same the previous Sunday when he had gone out. The Villa Borghese, the Piazza del Popolo, had implanted themselves in his consciousness with such an impression of longing that they were no more helpful than the four corners of his room. Yet, if he walked across the river and through Piazza Cavour toward Via Cola di Rienzo, the memory of his room took on the same quality of loss. At any moment, the telephone there might ring, offering him what he was searching for.

That Sunday he had taken a bus to some place on the outskirts of Rome. But at the end of the line he got back on the bus again and returned to Monte Mario where he climbed through the steep park behind Piazzale delle Medaglie d'Oro. He arrived at the Bar dello Zodiaco on a promontory with the Tiber almost directly below, twisting through the city's patchwork of trees and houses to the backdrop of the Alban hills. He walked around the white tower of the Astronomical Observatory, the landmark by which he located Marcello's house from the Pincio, and returned by a twisting, barbwire-fenced road along which couples of boys and girls watched until he passed, leaving them alone. He rejoined Via Trionfale near a group of tumble-down hovels and kitchen gardens and walked back into the city, past the street where Marcello lived.

A few minutes before eight, the acquaintance who had telephoned when Marcello was at the apartment telephoned again and asked Forrest to eat dinner with him. Forrest did not particularly want to; for the last hour he had not particularly wanted to do anything that was possible. But he did not want to eat alone and he lacked the presence of mind to think of an alternative. The rain had stopped and he put his indecision into wondering whether or not to wear a raincoat. He decided to go as he was.

It was the first dark of evening. Reflections of the streetlamps and neon signs glowed on the wet sidewalks and pavements. In Piazza di Spagna, as he was threading his way through the crowd and approaching the corner of Via Condotti, there, a yard before him, dressed in a dark blue, double-breasted gabardine suit, a blue and white striped shirt, a dark blue tie, stood Marcello.

The boy's hands were poised on the handle of a rolled-up black umbrella balanced on the sidewalk in front of him.

His clothes and stance were so unlike those that Forrest associated with him, and his presence in this place at this time was so unlikely, that Forrest thought he must be mistaken. Then their eyes met.

Forrest continued walking. Perhaps one of the men beside the boy was his father. But as soon as he was past, Marcello took a step after him.

"Ciao."

"What are you doing here?" Forrest asked.

"I have come to meet a friend who is to take me to see about a job."

Here on this corner, Forrest thought, where I used to see him arrive when he wanted to be picked up.

"But why are you meeting him here?"

"Because he works nearby."

A hollow, composed of disappointments that it was best not to put into words, rose in Forrest's chest. All his earlier suspicions returned full-blown. At what point, he wondered, did I cease to be a fool by being suspicious and begin to be a fool by believing?

Marcello seemed to have nothing more to say.

They stood in silence until Forrest, to cover his embarrassment, added:

"Well, remember to telephone me tomorrow if it rains."

He walked on, leaving Marcello on the corner, and did not look back.

The next day was one of the most beautiful of the year, even more beautiful than the Sunday before.

Forrest was awakened by a sound like the scraping of snow being shoveled in the street. The idea was incredible, but it was like no other sound. He rose and went to the window. Down below, a street sweeper was shoveling up trash and dust from the cobblestones.

The morning passed without Forrest's dressing. He made caffè latte in the kitchen and drank it wandering about the apartment in his robe, a thing he had not done before. Then he sat down and wrote to his father-in-law and to the man who had been in charge of his own Office since he had been away. He and the man had been in correspondence all along, but the main idea of the correspondence seemed to have been to keep him from worrying about business. Most of his information about what was going on had come from his father-in-law. Now he asked to be brought up to date on all their accounts in preparation for his return home. It was not due for a month yet, but he was feeling decisive and he might go back earlier. He had just finished when a telephone call came from his landlady. In the last weeks he had wished that he could stay on beyond the end of his three months, but he had not mentioned it to her. Now he was ready to leave at any moment. Her call clarified which set of intentions it is that you should not declare if you change your mind: neither. Otherwise, the call was confusing. She wanted to know if he intended to stay now that his three months were over. Which three months? He thought that they were over at the end of June and it was the beginning. She mentioned a jumble of terminations in July, August, September. He paid her by the month; there was no question about what he owed; and he could not tell what she was talking about. She said that there must be some misunderstanding. She would call back when her secretary was there.

It was a day to go swimming, but not at Ostia. In the early afternoon, without having eaten and without any appetite, he dressed and took a bus to Foro Italico at the foot of Monte Mario. The newspaper account that he read on the trip of the previous evening's rainstorm proved that, despite the beauty of the day, nature in Rome still has as devastating an effect on the city itself as it does on human relationships. After the long list of places that had been flooded, including the luggage room of the Trastevere railway station, there was: fallen electric wires, leaving filobuses lined up Indian file; trees uprooted in Via Cassia and Via Aurelia; an inundated busload of tourists rescued by firemen; a woman sent to the hospital by the collapse of an awning full of water on her head; fallen cornices; interrupted telephone service; collapsed buildings; extensive damage to crops and vineyards in the Castelli Romani. Lightning had struck the Palace of Justice, Castel Sant'Angelo, and the radio tower on Monte Mario.

The outdoor pool at Foro Italico was the most beautiful that Forrest had ever been in. There was a large crowd of people swimming and diving from the Olympic tower. Others were sunbathing on the red tile walks surrounding the pool. He stayed all afternoon, leaving only when the pool closed, and walked back through Prati, where he stopped for a long time at an outdoor café. He ate supper late at the trattoria on Via di Ripetta, across from a reunion party of soccer players. It was midnight when he got home.

A perfect day — and, like Saturday, perfectly lost.

And yet, as he was undressing in the empty apartment, he reminded himself that Saturday had given him two indelible memories: Marcello disconcertingly American and modern in his white khaki trousers and rainbow-striped raw silk shirt, and Marcello strangely nineteenth century in his too mature, cut-down-looking, double-breasted suit, his rolled-up umbrella balanced between his folded hands and the wet sidewalk, at eight o'clock at night in Piazza di Spagna, surrounded by the rush-hour traffic passing the corner of Via Condotti, the neon-colored twilight slowly closing in on him. The second image was like a photograph come across unexpectedly in one of the pushcarts of the antique dealers in Piazza Borghese; yet it was a sight that should rid him of any illusions if he were capable of being rid of them. That Sunday, however, it only helped to form in his mind the questions of a parent or of a possessive lover, neither of which positions he had a right to assume.

By Monday morning he had accepted the events of Saturday. He stayed in the apartment, but because he had tasks to do, not because there was still a need to wait around for telephone calls. Marcello, he felt sure, would be so ashamed of what had happened that it would be weeks before he returned. Sitting down at the dining room table, he wrote to everyone he could think of, beginning with his wife and ending with his mother in Ohio. It was as hot as it had been the day before, and he thought that after lunch he would go back to the piscina at Foro Italico.

At noon, he answered the doorbell. There stood Marcello in the blue coat and striped blue and white shirt of Saturday, and tan gabardine trousers. Perhaps it was only that his hair was newly cut, but he looked more like a twelve-year-old than ever. Even in the dark double-breasted jacket, it was difficult to picture him as anything nearer to a naval officer than a child playing one in a pantomime.

"I was near," he said, "so I didn't telephone."

Forrest was taken off guard by this unannounced appearance, so like the chance encounter in an unexpected place that he had long and unsuccessfully wished for.

"You look hot."

"I've been going around all morning about my job," Marcello said. "May I take off my coat?"

He smiled as apologetically as he had that first day when he asked permission to use the comb in the bedroom.

"Here is the paper from the shop sending me to the school," he added, handing Forrest a letter. "And here is the list of equipment I need for the school that I have been going around to find."

Forrest looked at the letter: Scuola di Parrucchiere. It was a joke of a job for Marcello to have.

"Who pays for the school?"

"The company that makes the beauty products that the shop uses. But you have to be sent there by the shop."

"How long do you go?"

"Two weeks."

Marcello gave a smile of joyous wickedness.

"Then I start to work. Fortunately for the customers, I will only be allowed to wash their hair."

The smile faded slowly. His eyes dropped to the floor, then looked up. His voice, when he spoke again, was lower.

"Let's go in the other room."

The white socks that he was wearing, when they appeared in the process of undressing, had turned red from perspiration and the cheaply dyed leather of his shoes. Then he peeled off the socks. His feet were streaked the color of blood, as though he had walked through barbed-wire to get there.

The sight of them made him laugh; but Forrest, the last of his caution gone, embraced him with an abandon that he had not known before.

Later the breeze, coming through the closed outside blinds, billowed the white curtains into the room where they lay nude on the bed, not touching.

"At least you don't get cold now."

"No."

Marcello said the word softly. Forrest sat up and looked at him.

"Your big toe," he said, 'is longer than any of the others."

"Is that wrong?"

"No, but the second toe is usually longer. I have only seen the big toe longer in the drawings of athletes on Greek vases."

"Then I have classical toes."

"Yes."

"Then I do not need to worry about them."

"No."

Marcello's body, with the muscles faintly and clearly lined on, had the same proportion and definition as that of a youth on a Greek vase. Forrest lay down again.

"I'm glad that you came this morning."

"So am I."

"You are very faithful."

Marcello's face focused into attention.

"Faithful to whom?"

"Oh, to yourself. But that faithfulness is the most valuable."

"Why?"

"It lasts after other people."

Marcello smiled and closed his eyes.

"You are really extraordinary," Forrest added.

"I am not. Why do you say that? I am an ordinary boy."

"Perhaps."

Forrest placed his face against the ordinary boy's neck, close to the sepia constellation, and inhaled the clean odor of his perspiration. He felt like going to sleep.

Marcello, grinning, lifted the wrist on which he wore his watch, looked at it, and said with a wordless movement of his eyes: It is time for me to go.

"Where did you get that watch?" Forrest asked.

"Ninì gave it to me."

"In America, girls do not give expensive presents to boys."

"Ah then, I shall never go to America."

"I preferred you without a watch. Where do you have to go, anyway?"

"I have to be at home to eat."

"Can't you eat with me?"

"It is difficult."

"I would like you to eat with me," Forrest said, "and I would like you to go with me to the piscina at Foro Italico."

"All right."

"All right what?"

He had expressed his wishes without a thought that they would be fulfilled. An agreement nonplussed him.

"All right, I will go with you to the piscina."

"When?"

"Tomorrow morning, if possible. When I know, I will telephone you. All right?"

Marcello looked at his watch, smiled, and moved to a sitting position.

"Shall we get dressed now?"

The French cuffs of the blue and white striped shirt were fastened with imitation cameo cuff links. Forrest asked what cuff links are called in Italian.

"Gemelli. The same word as twins. Because there are two of them."

When he was dressed, Marcello asked permission to use the telephone. Forrest enjoyed listening to his conversation. He was talking to his girl friend.

"I am at the school now," he said, "but I am leaving. Shall we meet each other and walk to the bus together after dinner?"

As soon as Marcello was gone, Forrest felt a panic-stricken desire to run after him.

It was the same desire that he had felt the day he had learned that Marcello lived on Via Giordano Bruno. But how much stronger it had become. He looked around him and could find no recognizable meaning in the world he was left alone in. The letters he had written an hour before, his plans for the afternoon, seemed memories from another life. He felt as though a part of his own self had departed, leaving him only half able to breathe or to move. On his birthday, he had thought: Marcello is seventeen and I am thirty-four, exactly twice his age, a coincidence that will never occur again. His anxiety seemed to be a panic-stricken extension of this thought.

He longed so strongly to escape his maimed condition that he was reminded of Giordano Bruno's statement that an animal, if it were aware of the difference between its condition and that of man, would prefer death, if death would put it on the way to man's estate, to the life that held it in its lower one.

He was at the door when the telephone rang. It was the landlady's secretary. Her call clarified the question of the apartment. The landlady had found a tenant who was willing to lease the place beginning in August; did he want to keep the apartment through July, or to renew his lease through September?

"July."

He hung up, thinking of something else. He had been reduced to this state by seeing Marcello twice in three days. If they saw each other more often, it might become even worse. Yet what alternative did he have to hoping that Marcello would telephone him tomorrow?

CHAPTER 7

The warm weather, which irritated most Romans, improved the Sicilian temper of Marcello's father. He listened in silence to the announcement that his son made that day at the dinner table about his prospective job. Marcello knew that his father's silence was ominous, but he preferred it to the storm he had expected. During the meal, his sisters plied him with questions about the school. He answered reluctantly. His mind was less on the school than on Forrest. He was glad that they had made up. The unforeseen encounter in Piazza di Spagna had thrown his pride. He had realized, at the prospect of losing Forrest's good opinion, that it had given him a new confidence. And the fact that Forrest's good opinion had been in danger of being lost for no good reason, and when he had done no wrong, had increased its value. Forrest's feeling for him had some resemblance to family affection; he recognized in it the faithfulness that the American attributed to him, and also a solitariness and an independence that he knew from himself when he took his long walks. There had been nothing that he could do about it that night; he had had to wait for Norma's fidanzato; but as he watched Forrest walking away, he had promised himself that if they made up he would see Forrest as often as possible.

His reluctance to answer his sisters' questions had another cause: he was not sure that anything would come of his going to the hairdressing school. Norma's fidanzato, it had turned out, did not personally know the owner of the parrucchiere shops. He had spoken to the manager of the unit where he worked and that man had spoken to the owner. When they arrived at the office in the hotel, there were two girls and another boy waiting in the foyer. The secretary told Norma's fidanzato that he did not need to wait, that Marcello could keep the appointment alone.

When he entered the office, in his turn after the others, there behind the desk sat the man who had picked him up the first time in an automobile in the Villa Borghese;. The man did not evince the least surprise. He asked Marcello to sit down and said that he was glad to see him again. The job, he explained, required personality rather than skill; Marcello had the required attribute. Nevertheless, he would need some training. The secretary, on his way out, would give him a letter to the beauticians' school.

"Wait for me outside," he added. "Since we live in the same direction, I'll drive you home."

They took a route that brought them first to the man's apartment, a different apartment from the one he had taken Marcello to before.

"Come in a minute," he said. "I have a dog that I want to show you."

The dog was a Yorkshire terrier. It ran in like an animated dust mop, looking back over its shoulder anxiously as though it expected someone to attack it from behind. The man greeted it, petted it, then said to Marcello:

"Would you like something to drink?"

"No, thank you."

"Would you like to go to bed?"

"No. Tonight, no."

"Really? You don't have to worry about the job."

"I don't feel like it," Marcello said. And then, realizing that this would not suffice for the future if the man insisted: "Perhaps I'm too old for that sort of thing."

The man's half-smile reflected his own.

"Yes, perhaps you're too old. Well, I'll take you home."

He insisted on driving Marcello, despite his protests that it was not necessary, as far as Largo Trionfale. The Yorkshire terrier, who came along, barked at him from the window of the automobile as he walked away.

He had known in the office, as soon as the man offered him a ride, that he no longer wanted to go to bed with someone whom he felt no attraction or affection for, especially someone who felt no affection for him. As he passed the empty elementary school building on the corner of Via Giordano Bruno and turned toward home, he no longer was reassured by his old sense of being himself because he was the one common element connecting the different spheres of his existence. He felt lost. He wished that he dared to turn around and go to Forrest's apartment. He wanted to be near someone who cared for him, to be made love to, and to drive away his premonition that the more things he learned and the more people he encountered the less significance everything would have. The endless number of jobs that there might be to work in and the endless number of unknown people that there might be to meet were impersonal and dismaying. He arrived home glad, at least, to leave behind him the loneliness of the street. Franco let him in and jumped into his arms. His mother was in the kitchen. His sisters were setting the supper table. Franco asked him to fix the broken chain on his bicycle. Fortunately, he changed his clothes to do this and when his father came in he had no idea that Marcello had been out, or he might have kept him in the house on Sunday.

He and Ninì rode to the beach the next day in the red Alfa Romeo. Her oldest brother had returned from his honeymoon and offered to take them. It was not what they had planned, and not what he had gotten the money for, but the disappointment of not being alone was made up for by the excitement of riding in the luxurious automobile. At the Nuova Pineta, the brother rented two cabins, one for himself and Marcello, one for his wife and sister, and paid for everything. Marcello talked to him as they changed, then hurried to find Ninì. He wanted very much for the day to live up to his expectations. He had gone that morning and had his hair cut, and he was wearing his new bathing slip. He had had to bring it and his towel in the shoddy airplane bag that he used to carry his gym clothes to and from school in, but on the beach that did not matter.

He found Ninì walking alone by the water. The sand along the shore was as black as axle grease. The bathers who lay on it looked like swimmers greased to conquer the English Channel. Almost no one was swimming, but a group of boys were running and diving parallel to the shore where the water was only a few inches deep. A number of them had skinned faces. Ninì expressed her disapproval of this pastime.

"Let's go back among the cabins," she said when her brother and his wife came down to the water. "The sand is nicer there. And I want to be in the shade so I won't be sunburned."

As he lay stretched out in the sun, facing her where she sat against the side of a cabin in the shade, he saw that in a bathing suit her figure was much better than he had imagined that it would be. His concupiscence of the night before returned and he wished that he could make love to her. He did not know how it would be possible, but he knew that since he had become friends with her his type had changed. The girls who caught his eye in the crowd were no longer the tall, thin-faced ones. They were no longer girls who, as it happened, resembled him, but ones who resembled Ninì. They were often prettier than she was; but this greater beauty did not make them more attractive; and it was the traits that they shared with her, rather than those with which they surpassed her, that excited him.

What he was excited by when he was with Forrest was something else; it was as far from the emotion he felt for Ninì as the dislike he had experienced for the man last evening was from the pleasure he knew with Forrest. A sharp, new sense of the mystery of identity penetrated him as he lay there on the sand with the heat of the sun bearing down on him. Out of the thousands of people on the beach, there were only a few whose appearances he liked, and fewer whom he would want to know, narrowing down to the one opposite him in whom he sensed the surprising importance that another person can have, the importance that had existed for him in his mother and father when he was small, but that had disappeared, and that he had not imagined until now could exist outside the family.

Touching Ninì's foot, looking at the line where her hair met her neck, noticing the mole on her thigh, he entered, without conscious thought, some understanding of the process by which love, when the world expands, limits responses and makes intensity possible. The loneliness and insignificance that he had felt the previous night disappeared behind the girl facing him. For a moment he wondered what he would do if she again should become indifferent to him as she had been that first night at the dance. But he was reassured by seeing in her face, at the same time so childish and so mature, what had previously been concealed from him: that the attraction she felt for him, like the attraction he felt for her, was reinforced by the ingenuity of physical desire.

It was not true, as he had believed, that one thing about a girl—her appearance, her character, her actions—makes her attractive; it was the combination. How foolish he had been when he was content to stay with the crowd with Nini. He wished that he was alone with her now in the cabin with the door shut. And he wondered how she had foreseen what he would feel. For he felt that he no longer wanted to leave Rome and go to sea when he finished school. He wanted to have his own home, like his family's, but without his father, and with himself in the position of saying fairly how things should be done. He would not be ill-tempered or ugly. He would not abuse his power. And he would not do the things that he did now.

Talking to Nini that Sunday afternoon, he felt that he did not want to do anything in the future that he could not tell her, and he was glad again that he had refused the shopowner the night before. Nini already knew an acceptable story about Forrest, so that would be all right if Forrest would still see him. Forrest was no competition to his feelings for Nini, anyway. It would be a long time before they could properly make love. His and Forrest's friendship would make everything better. And the next morning when he said to Forrest that he would never go to America, he smiled to himself to think that it was to Forrest, jokingly, that he first put into words what he had felt lying on the beach with Nini, and that he would be able to say it to her by telling her what he had replied when Forrest had asked him where he had gotten his watch.

He was not so sure at the dinner table—when he was telling his sisters about the school, in face of his father's silence—that he would never again feel trapped in Rome and need to console himself with the idea that he would escape as soon as possible. He wondered what he would do if that time should come. But he put it to the back of his mind. He had long ago learned to take advantage of his father's silences while they lasted.

That afternoon, Rome began to seem to him a great net, not that he was trapped in, but that he was weaving across the city, thread by thread, on autobuses. He took a number 23 and a C to go to the school; afterward, a C and a number 64 to meet Nini. The next morning he accompanied her to work on the number 70 that they had returned on the night before; then, after going home to get his bathing slip, a number 32 to the piscina where he met Forrest at eleven at the ticket booth beside the entrance.

At the pool, as they were walking up the steps behind the diving tower, which went from beside the bar and restaurant to a higher level where there was a separate pool for children, Forrest made a reference to the time when he would have to leave Italy and go back to work.

"When might you leave?"

"Perhaps at the end of the month."

"So soon?"

"I am due back at work shortly afterward. And the lease on the apartment is finished then."

They walked around the children's pool and the group of sunbathers and back down the steps. When they were once more beside the diving tower, Marcello said:

"But you can get another, smaller apartment and stay."

"Yes. I can probably even stay another month in the same apartment. But by then I have to be at work. And I've things to do first."

Except for once, they had never talked of Forrest's family and life in America, and Marcello did not know if Forrest's indecision was because he was still disappointed in him. But he did not know what else he could say.

"In any case," Forrest added, "I have to go soon."

He tried to do whatever Forrest wanted that morning. They walked around the pool, swam, and walked around the pool again.

When it was half past noon, Forrest said:

"I don't suppose that you can eat with me today?"

"It is better that I eat with the family. But, if you like, I will meet you at the apartment this afternoon."

He took the number 32 home. After dinner, he accompanied Ninì part-way to work on one bus and changed to another for the school. He also changed buses coming back from the school to Forrest's apartment.

"There is a milky way of small flat moles along your back, like the constellation on your face," Forrest told him when they were undressing.

"And that is not classical?"

"No."

"But you like them?"

"Oh, yes, I like them."

"Very well."

When they had made love, Forrest said:

"Yesterday afternoon I took a walk while the maid was cleaning. In the window of a jewelry store I saw a pair of gold cuff links. They were very beautiful. Perhaps they will be a good present for you."

"Perhaps—"

He felt more free to speak to Forrest, but he still had trouble making a request. Gold cuff links for him, however, would not do when he had given ceramic ones to Ninì.

"—if you would like it just as well, I would prefer something else."

"What?"

"A bag."

"A bag! What do you mean, a bag?"

"To take to the beach. I have only the one I have used for two years to take my gym clothes to school in. It's worn and it smells like the gym. And it is so small that if I want to take a lunch to the beach for the day it crushes everything."

"Have you seen a bag that you want?"

"I haven't looked. But they are easy to find. There are sure to be good ones at La Rinascente."

The shopping trip was even more of a pleasure than the one for the shirt. They did not have to go from place to place. His only difficulty in making up his mind on the mezzanine of La Rinascente was to know if the bag he wanted might not cost more than Forrest would like to pay.

"This one? Or maybe that?"

"Whichever you prefer."

"The larger one isn't too expensive?"

"No."

It was handsome: a green canvas bag trimmed with blue leather, deeper than it was wide, with looped leather handles at the top.

This time he found it easy to say thank you for something that he had asked for.

He himself, in his turn, was asked for something at the end of the week.

He should have known that his father's silence had gone on too long for it to end mildly. Claudia had said:

"Lello, why don't you ask Papa for something? For a new suit or for permission to do something? He's just waiting for you to ask him."

"So he can refuse me."

"Maybe not. And it will be better about your working for someone else if you ask him for something. Otherwise, he'll be meaner and meaner until he forces you to give in."

"I'll not ask him for anything."

"He's buying both Norma and me new dresses. I'm sure the deal with the friends of Signor Tocci is going through. Now is the right time."

"Let him offer me something. I'm his son. He hasn't spoken to me for a week."

There had been enough else to occupy him. He had seen Forrest four times that week. Only for a minute to say hello the day after they bought the bag, but for an hour the day after that. He had seen Ninì each morning or evening, riding part of the way to work with her, or meeting her after work and accompanying her home. At the apartment at night, using his sisters as guinea pigs, he had practiced the instructions he had been given at the school. His father had seen him doing this, but he waited until Sunday dinner before he brought up the subject.

It was raining. Everyone, trapped in the apartment, was restless and busy.

Only Franco was missing. He had left the day before for a month at a summer colony for children, run by the Church, on the beach at Santa Severa, north of Rome.

To make up for Franco's absence, his father's sister and her husband, who still lived near Saint Peter's where they had lived when Renzo was alive, were at the apartment for dinner.

Marcello was standing beside the parakeets' cage, which had been brought in from the wet terrace and was hanging in the L-shaped hallway, a space for washing and ironing, that ran back of the kitchen. He had spent the morning, at Norma's request, building a house for the parakeets. The finished house was attached to the cage and held the nest, in which there were now three greenish-white eggs.

Turning from the cage, he looked out of the window and down at an oleander tree in the rain on the far side of the street. In the kitchen, his aunt was talking to his sisters, who were making a great deal of noise and confusion trying to prepare zuppa inglese. Unlike their mother, who was tired of their nonsense, she joined in their enthusiasm and asked them questions, just as she used to join in his enthusiasm for building model ships and let him explain the process to her as though it were what she had always wanted to know. He had often wondered why his aunt was so unlike her brother; but now, hearing her voice in the kitchen, he noticed that her tone was very much like his father's when he was playing with Franco, very much like his father's tone had been with him in the past.

The oleander tree down below in the rain reminded him of those days. He had owned a bicycle, the last present that his father had lovingly given him, but he had never gone out of the neighborhood on it, just as Franco never went out of the neighborhood on his bicycle now. There had been a row of oleander bushes outside the window of the apartment where they lived, and in the summer he had spent hours watching the ants that were always swarming over the trunks and branches. He wondered if there were ants on the wet tree down below or if they only came out in the sun. Everything was better when it didn't rain. He had hoped to have a whole day at the beach with Ninì, either by themselves or with his sisters. But she had telephoned earlier and said that since the weather was bad she was going to Palestrina with her aunt to visit relatives and would not be back until late. Because of the rain he was not even going to see her for a walk. And the new beach bag was under the bed in his room, still unused.

His aunt came out of the kitchen and said:

"They've finished, Lello. I think we're ready to eat. Come to table."

He knew why his aunt and uncle were there. His uncle ran a wine and oil store, but he had investments and connections in the building business. He had been a friend of Signor Tocci's when his father first knew him and had helped when his father had received the floor tile contract that had enabled him to start his own business. Claudia was probably right; his father must be about to make money again and he would be nicer. Perhaps if he were to go to work for his father now he would be paid. And he decided that if the promise of the job at the parrucchiere shop came to nothing, and if his father would make some friendly gesture to him, offer him a pair of shoes, or even say that he needed his help, he would go to work with him for the summer.

At the table, he learned that his sisters had been telling his aunt and uncle about Nìnì.

"So you've gotten over being shy with girls," his uncle said.

"I was never shy."

"Oh, yes, you were."

"When?"

"When you lived in our neighborhood. You were in love with a girl named Anna Maria. Her family lived near my store and you used to ask me to let you ride to work with me to go by her house. But if she was on the street you would get down under the dashboard and wouldn't come back up until I assured you that she was no longer there."

His sisters, who had never heard this story before, burst into laughter.

"When I wanted to know if you were afraid of her, you asked me if I knew Richard Cœur de Lion. You said that you were his brother. And when I asked if that meant that you were as brave as he was, you said that you were his brother, not he, and that his brother was another person."

While the rest of the family were laughing at this, his father took advantage of the opportunity to say:

"Well, Richard Cœur de Lion's brother is a brave man now. He's not afraid to wash his sisters' hair in the evenings or to work in a shop full of hairdressers."

His aunt, as though she had not heard his father, said:

"I still see Anna Maria. Last fall, when you won the hundred-meter dash for your school, she came in the store and told me how proud she was of you."

"He has a girl friend who's given him a watch and who takes him to the beach in an Alfa Romeo," his father continued, "and he's going to have a full-time job and pay rent at home."

"Papa," said Claudia.

"His rent won't be as high as the salary I pay the employee at the kiln who will do the work he could do, but it will offset part of it. And every little bit helps."

"I don't have a job yet, Papa," Marcello said.

"No, but I have a new employee, so your rent has started. Do you have three thousand lire to give me this week?"

"No, Papa."

"I thought not. Well, we'll put it down to your account and you will pay me when you do have a job."

CHAPTER 8

Forrest had been awake since five o'clock. At ten, he could stand it no longer. He took his bathing suit and a towel, put on his dark glasses, and went out. At Porta del Popolo, he caught a bus to the Stazione Termini. There was a train to Santa Severa in half an hour. Until the time for departure, he sat in a wooden-benched compartment, watching the Roman families arriving on their way to the sea for the day.

Outside Rome, in a final underlining of the absence of floral seasons, the hillsides were blooming with mimosa and broom, just as they had bloomed in the spring. Events do repeat themselves. Forrest, when he was first married, had been given a gold fountain pen by his wife. It was a well-meant gift, but he put it away and did not use it because he always lost fountain pens. Then, at his wife's insistence, he took it out, used it, and lost it.

Now he had learned again that the value of gold is not real. He had wanted to give Marcello the pair of gold cuff links because they would be of permanent value and would leave some reminder of him in Marcello's possession after he was gone. But to Marcello, without friends who wore gold cuff links, their value was not real. Whatever "value" they possessed could only be realized by his selling them, turning them into money, no longer having them. And so he did not want them. Getting something that he wanted was what pleased him, not getting something of value, not gain for gain's sake. He lived in a practical world, direct in its desires and easily corrupted; but he had not been corrupted. He would rather have had the canvas bag of the family sitting across the carriage.

How strange that I cannot give him something of value by giving him gold, Forrest thought. By giving him money, which is the symbol of gold, I can give something that he wants. But by giving him gold, which is the symbol of value, I cannot. It is what can be used and will disappear that he wants. His life is still that far from the impractical and satiated; the conventionality he longs for is still that unsophisticated. But this is not because the society that he lives in is simple. Romans certainly love gold. And he certainly loves money. But he prefers choosing what he likes, not what is expensive. And how many people dare to do that now when they have the chance to do otherwise? Who nowdays quite believes that value is not equivalent to price?

Nearly everyone in Forrest's compartment got out at Palo-Cerveteri. There were only half a dozen people left. He and a family of three descended at Santa Severa. The small station was shaded by trees and surrounded by a flower garden. But the dusty road that made an elbow turn from the station, past a single house to the highway, was bare to the blazing midday sun. The paved highway was even more glaring and hot. At a wineshop, he stopped and asked which was the way to the bathing establishments on the beach. There were several dirt roads leading off through pine and eucalyptus trees toward the sea. All of them, the man replied; whichever you prefer.

He took the first, leading straight to a ruined medieval castle, the one noticeable object in the flat summer landscape between the sea and the inland hills.

The castle had become a farm. Skirting it, he went through a bog that resembled a pig yard but was full of geese. A wooden fence separated the bog from a pasture of cows. He ducked under a corner of the fence and came out on the beach. Before him, there was sand more nearly white than any that he had seen before in Italy, and breakers like those on the Atlantic coast. Tents and umbrellas stretched along the beach to his right. A caravan of Arabs and Tartars seemed to have settled there, not a summer colony of Italian children. But the beach was not crowded. And a pleasant breeze blew in from the sea.

Almost at once, as he started up the shore, he saw Marcello in his black bathing slip, standing on a dune, framed against eucalyptus trees and the sky. At his side there was a thin, dried-up man whom Forrest assumed to be his father. They were drinking from paper cups, something out of a Thermos bottle. Without looking again toward them, he continued up the water's edge in what would be the direction of Marcello's gaze if he had not turned. He did not know whether he hoped Marcello would see him or not. But if Marcello did, it would be at a distance, walking away. The only thing left of his reasonableness was the ridiculous decision that, if the distance was to be shortened, Marcello would have to shorten it.

At first there were no bath cabins, then two groups of them, one after the other. At each establishment he received the same answer: Completely full. He walked all the way to the end of the beach, to what seemed to be another locality. There, on the dunes, a cement-block restaurant sat behind a reed-roofed terrace on which people were eating. He cut up from the sand, through the dust and dried plants and flowers, like those on a sun-baked Midwestern field, and sat down at a table.

Forking it into his mouth in the same slow steady manner that he had walked up the beach, he ate a great mound of spaghetti alle vongole. The one thing as the other, he did out of the compulsion not to do something else, not to look back, not to face the decision that he would have to face when he was not eating. There were only Italians in the noisy half-naked crowd around him, not another tourist, probably not another non-Roman. The scene was a vignette, in fact, of his position among Romans. There were couples, hairy men across from plump women; and families, endless children jumping in and out of their folding chairs as often as if they were playing tag; but not another person at a table alone. He followed the spaghetti with abbacchio arrosto.

In the week that had followed the previous rainy Sunday, as in the week that had preceded it, he had been to bed with Marcello three times. As he had feared, his state was worse than ever. He could not figure out why the increased appointments did not make him happier. He was happy all the time that they were together. But his worst night had been after they had gone to the pool in the morning and to bed in the afternoon. That evening he had not known where he was. With despair, he realized that it would have been better to have caught sight of Marcello at the pool with his friends than it had been to go there with him. He had wanted to enter the boy's life, but he had only managed to draw the boy a tiny way into his own. And he was outside any life at all.

Yet, close to him, and connected to his existence at a single point, was a whole world that it seemed possible for him to enter. He lusted for all of it. Its streets. Its houses. Its hours of dinner and supper. Its arguments. Its boredoms. The faces of its least beautiful members. He possessed all of it, incomprehensibly, in a hostage. But it was like possessing a masterpiece in a language that he could not read. Like possessing a book by touch. A painting by taste. A sculpture by smell. For the first time, he understood a friend of his wife's who had become rich and famous overnight and had been reduced by this good luck to an ecstasy of misery.

No frustration quite equals the frustration of possessing what you cannot comprehend possessing. The night after the morning at the pool and the afternoon at the apartment, he had wandered about the streets repeating to himself the tag line of the story of the man who declares himself ready to go to hell: But, sir, where do you think you are?

He was nowhere, and it suddenly occurred to him that this was what his wife had felt when they were traveling together. The idea was such a revelation that he longed for her to be there so he could tell her. Then the ridiculousness of the desire struck him. Seated alone in the midst of the tables full of diners, he burst out laughing. The nearer people stopped with forks held before their faces, as though they expected him to run amuck. She had needed something familiar to hold onto, just as he did now. She had been unable to comprehend possessing him where everything was unfamiliar. That was why they had fought so much: nothing is so familiar as familiar discord.

It was intolerably hot under the reed matting. He got his check, paid it, and started back down the beach. This time he discovered that although there were no cabins for rent, he could, by paying a hundred and fifty lire, change in one of the bright-colored tents. He had no beach bag, but after he had taken off his shirt and trousers he rolled his shoes up in them and carried the bundle under his arm.

He kept his eyes focused a long way ahead as he walked, trying to catch sight of Marcello and his family before he reached them. Suddenly, he dropped to the sand as though shot. The group was several yards ahead. They were at the back of the beach, on the edge of the dunes, so they were not really too near. But when he sat up he looked for a long time at the water, not daring to turn around.

Then he lay down, rolled over on his stomach, and peered in the direction where they were.

Marcello was lying on his back, three girls seated around him. They were all talking and laughing. One of the girls covered up Marcello's face with her wide-brimmed straw hat. Another, reaching out her hand slowly, slowly, jerked a hair out of his chest. Forrest did not see the beach bag and did not know which of the groups of people in the dunes behind them contained the rest of the family. But he remembered that Marcello had only two sisters. The third girl must be the one he had seen in the photograph, the one who had the same birthday that he had. As he tried to decide which she was, he realized for the first time how ridiculous the prediction in the horoscope was, "magnificent romantic opportunity in the late afternoon," if it was supposed to be applicable to both him and her.

He strained his eyes to discover the man he had seen earlier drinking from the Thermos with Marcello. He did not find him and looked for a boy the age of Marcello's younger brother. There were dozens of them. Their names and voices filled the air over the beach. Then Marcello and the girls jumped up. They walked away from him at first, on the back of the sandy stretch, going to speak to someone in the dunes. Then they ran down to the water, still farther away, and waded out into the shallow breakers.

Forrest stood up. Motion was necessary. If he did not go in one direction, he would go in the other. He walked back toward the restaurant. When he reached a place where there was a crowd of people, he laid down his bundle of clothes and waded out beyond the breakers as the others had. The water was cool and pleasant. Around him, people were splashing each other like children in a bathtub. A few were floating in relaxed and strange positions on inflated inner tubes. All of them were having a good time. There was no sign of the frustrated disappointment usual among American families on outings for pleasure. They were happy. And he realized that he was, too.

He came out of the water and lay down with his head on his bundle. He was farther away from Marcello and the girls than he had been before, but near enough to see them when they came back to the beach. As he watched them merge into the crowd near the dunes, he felt that his situation was the same as it would have been if he had been in love with one of the girls, or if he had been going to bed with boys all his life. His pleasure and bewilderment had very little to do with his being out of his depths. It had everything to do with the separation between him and the life around him. The trouble was that he was not Roman.

The idea calmed him so much, together with the food, the water, and the sun, that he nearly went to sleep. The sound of a familiar voice, close up, brought him out of his bemusement. Marcello was directly behind him, threading his way through the crowd on the beach, calling in an authoritative tone:

"No, Franco. Don't bother Mamma. I'll go with you. Here, take my hand. Don't run."

Forrest felt as happy as though he had played a trick on someone. He laughed aloud, not as he had in the restaurant, but quietly, almost to himself, his mouth close against the bundle. The person he had played a trick on, however, was himself. With a return of reason, he saw how hopeless it was that, simply because he had known that Marcello was coming here, he had been unable not to follow him. The least that he could do was to leave now and save himself the further indignity of skulking around the beach all afternoon, skirting an encounter that could only be uncomfortable for him and for Marcello. He had not had the foresight on his arrival to look carefully at the schedule of returning trains; he thought that there was one at five-thirty. He stood up, anxious to change into his clothes and get to the station as quickly as possible. If only, since he had stayed this long without being seen, he could get away unnoticed.

He returned by a different route from the one he had taken on arriving, through the lanes in the white-trunked eucalyptus grove. On the highway, he stopped at the osteria where he had inquired earlier and drank a quartino of cold white wine. When he arrived at the station, he saw that the train he remembered had been at fifteen-thirty, not five-thirty. It was five-forty-five, anyway. The next train was in an hour.

A caged bird was singing on the wall of the station. Near it, a small boy was playing among the flower beds with a string and a kitten. He smiled at Forrest.

"Gioco gattino."

Together, they amused themselves with the cat. People began to arrive at the station. First a trickle. Then more and more. Forrest returned and looked at the schedule. The next train was the last until late evening. Everyone would be returning on it

He wondered at which end of the station he should wait to avoid encountering Marcello and his family. Then he decided that he would watch for them. The narrow stretch of platform between the tracks and the fenced-in flower plots was small enough, but the entrance to the station was a single gate through which everyone had to arrive. He stood himself against the wall of the building, facing the gate. That way, unless they were already there, he would see where they went.

They came toward the end, when families were pouring through the gate in a slow, steady stream. The green and blue beach bag was in Marcello's hand. He was with the three girls, but Forrest still did not see his parents. The girls paused, turning back, perhaps looking for the older people. Suddenly, terrified of an encounter, Forrest decided not to wait and see which way they would go. He hurried toward the extreme front end of the platform. And in a short while, there they came, strolling the same way. Just Marcello and the girls, as far as Forrest could see. But this time there was no place for him to retreat. He pushed himself almost into the middle of a family at the end of a baggage cart and waited. Marcello paused and put down the beach bag. He and the three girls, silent now, lined themselves up against the concrete fence. For ten minutes they waited, a few yards apart.

The trip back was a nightmare. There were no seats; there was hardly room to stand in the aisles. The train stopped in every station and restless hordes of people pushed their way in and out of the corner that Forrest was trapped in. He did not know from one minute to the next whom he was going to find himself face to face with. For a climax, the train arrived in Rome at a terminus that he had never seen before. No more stops. Stazione Tiburtina. Everyone out.

He was relieved to find a bus in front of the station with a destination on it that he recognized. He boarded it without a care that the destination was not near to the apartment. The important thing was to escape. He descended at Piazza Colonna and drank a negroni in the first bar that he came to. Potato chips and olives were sufficient food. The nearest approach to being a Roman was to cease to be himself. And each negroni peeled off a layer of awareness. He ordered another.

Standing next to him at the counter was a girl. She was an Italian of a different type from those he had seen at the beach all afternoon. Tall and thin, dressed in a beige, black-trimmed suit, she was beautiful in a way that girls seldom were in New York. As she reached in front of him for a potato chip, she smiled. He had often noticed that the girls at the Spanish Steps, not those who sat but those who walked briskly up and down, had this particular combination of simplicity and elegance. They impressed him as much as the women on Fifth Avenue had impressed him when he first came to New York. He returned her smile and offered her the olives.

How pleasant it would be, he thought, to spend the evening with her. It would take him back into the normal world, away from the nightmare of the afternoon. Those fast-walking girls at the Steps had always seemed unapproachable; but here this one was, standing still, alone. He might even be able to make love to her. He said that it had been a beautiful day. She looked surprised, but agreed. No, she was not a Roman. She was from Parma, but she worked in Rome. Where was he from and what did he do? She was so pleasant that he believed when he asked her to have dinner with him that she was going to accept. She looked at him for a moment as though making up her mind. Then she said that she had an engagement.

He was alone and did not want to be. But, except for the moment, it was not from lack of opportunities. Of all cities, Rome is the loneliest, because in no other city is the possibility of not being alone so omnipresent. He had refused an invitation to dinner that evening with the woman who had introduced him to the cardinal and who was in the city for the weekend from Positano. When, after a third negroni, he started walking up Via del Tritone, two women accosted him in the same block. If he was alone, it was because he seemed to have developed a talent for wanting the impossible. And the desire to be with his wife, which he had felt that afternoon, returned stronger than ever.

All up the street, people offered themselves to his gaze with the same insistence as the buildings and landscape. Whatever reason it had been that had made Marcello set eyes on him, it worked for endless others. He had once thought the air of Rome permissive. It was more than that. It caressed him as the sunlight did in the daytime, confusing touch and sight. In the dark around him, everything was as clear and full as the sound of Italian vowels, as rich and sweet as the *a* and *u* when they joined, double but single, each time that Marcello said Cla-udia, or the father at the trattoria called his son, Ma-uro.

A shadowed tree caught a shaft of light. An obelisk appeared and vanished behind a building. Without his knowing why, the sight of the moon over Via Sistina made him burst into tears.

He was drunk. But he talked with romantic soberness to himself. If only he could have been born in Rome and grown up there, how happy he would be. The idea was as joyous as the moon in the sky. But it brought the tears back to his eyes. Why was he happy in Rome, even when he was unhappy? He could imagine killing himself to become a part of the Roman earth. But he did not want to die in Rome. He wanted to be born there. And he decided that in his next incarnation he would be. He would be born as a Roman bird or cat. No, they were too difficult to comprehend without making them human. But, if Giordano Bruno is right, and when you are more deeply moved by the sight of some other thing you do not suffer the pangs of death, then, perhaps, as a Roman boy.

He had reached the top of the Spanish Steps. In the moonlight, the white expanse was like the grand staircase of an opera house.

He leaned on the balustrade; someone was at his elbow, asking for a match.

It was no one whom Forrest had ever seen before. Not one of the boys who had come to the apartment, looking for Robert. And not one of the students who were always hanging out at the Steps. It was a type that he associated with the night he had made his way up the dark street with Robert near Campo dei Fiori and heard the unknown voice calling, "Avanti, vieni qua!" A full-eyed type that he had seen on walks in Trastevere. Un romano di Roma.

"I don't smoke."

The boy pretended not to have known that he was addressing a foreigner.

"Oh, excuse me. I thought that you were Italian."

"I am," Forrest said. "I am Roman."

"Ah, you are Roman!" The boy laughed and threw an arm about Forrest's shoulder. "A real Roman. Good, good."

"I was born and raised in Rome."

"Benissimo. You speak Italian like a Roman. Benissimo."

He looked at Forrest with big, puppy-dog eyes, full of half-sly, half-humorous questioning. His hand was large, with Trasteverine fullness and color. He removed it from Forrest's shoulder and took a box of matches from his pocket.

"Look! There are matches." Smiling, he lit his cigarette and crumpled up the package. "My last."

Forrest was drunk. Later, he did not remember what he had said to the boy or exactly how the conversation had gotten around to their going to the apartment. It seemed to him that he had talked to and felt friendly for the dark red shirt as much as for the boy who was wearing it. He had been sure, too, that to take him home was the natural way out of the predicament that he was in. If he could not rid himself in one way of the illusion that he was involved in something unique and unfathomable, then he would rid himself of it in another.

His intention was definite. But it was backed by a confused desire. When they reached the apartment, everything was at odds. The situation left him feeling the next morning as he had felt when he had thought of Robert's going to bed with boys: what could be the possible point of it for him? If

he had had to pick up someone, he would have done better to have picked up one of the women on Via del Tritone.
How had he allowed himself to get into such a mess? He
remembered taking out a bottle of cognac and pouring
two glasses. He remembered the boy's drinking his, seated
across from him in one of the green chairs so that Forrest
could see that the zipper of his trousers was broken and the
fly closed with a safety pin. And he remembered the boy's
asking for money. Five thousand lire.

If he had pulled a knife, that would have been one thing;
but he had begged and combined threatening with begging, just as earlier he had combined slyness with smiling.
He remembered the boy's eating cioccolatini al liquore and
throwing the wrappers on the floor. He remembered taking
a shower. He took another in the morning. He did not remember what he had given the boy for the nothing that had
happened. His pockets were empty, and he wished that he
knew how much money he had had. His drunkenness had
left his body and mind soiled. He was full of calm self-dis-
gust. But the calmness had its value.

As long as it lasted. Which was until after Marcello's
visit. He came in the morning, as he had done once before,
to say hello on his way to the school. It was his last day, the
day that he was to be given his job and start to work. When
Forrest asked if his presence at Santa Severa the previous
afternoon had upset him, Marcello smiled and shook his
head, more unfathomable to Forrest than ever. He could
not help but contrast this simpleness with his own conduct
of the night before. He had not solved his problem.

Marcello had come to see him because he did not want
him to leave Rome. He sat on the sofa like a cat that comes
and sits in its master's apartment, knowing that its absence
makes the apartment less desirable and that the master may
go away. He made no demonstrations. He was not a dog.

He did not wag his tail and say: I love you. He was a cat who sat and, in his glance, reminded: If you love me, here I am to be loved. If my presence will make you stay, here is my presence. I want, in my way, what you want. I do not pretend that the barriers between us do not exist. Or that they can be removed. But I do not want you to leave.

They left the apartment together, Forrest taking his traveler's checks with him to go by the American Express. They parted when he went to change his money. He sat alone in the sun for a few minutes at the bottom of the Spanish Steps. When he returned to the apartment, by way of Via della Croce, where he bought fresh figs and prosciutto for his lunch, he had not been gone more than three-quarters of an hour. The front door was open. He had locked it, as he always did. Could the landlady be there? He went into the front room, through it to the dining room. There was no one in either room, but in the second the contents of his brief-case, which he had left open when he took out his traveler's checks, were scattered on the floor.

"Who's in here?" he demanded.

He hurried into his bedroom. The covers of the bed were thrown back. Someone had been searching beneath the mattress. The bedroom beyond, however, was undisturbed. He continued to circle the apartment until he reached the entrance hall again. At the front door, he saw what he had not noticed before: it had been forced. The lock was hanging from the wooden framework. He looked down the staircase. He saw no one, but he felt certain that the thief had been in the apartment while he was making his tour and had just escaped down the stairs.

Forrest went around the apartment, checking. He was not thorough, but he found nothing missing. He felt extraordinarily calm, calmer than he had been earlier in the morning. He was entering the life of Rome, whether or not pleasantly, and whether or not in a manner that he was capable of dealing with. His calm disappeared only when he sat down to eat his lunch. The hand in which he was holding his fork suddenly began to shake.

He rose and walked about the apartment, looking again to see if anything was missing. In the kitchen, he put the food in the refrigerator and poured himself another glass of wine. He drank the wine, walking around, then sat down in the chair where the boy had been sitting the night before. Between the cushion and the side, there was a package of cigarettes. He took one out and lit it.

When the maid arrived, she advised him not to inform the police.

"No good will come of it," she said, as though she were reciting a prayer. "They will only demand a list of the Italians that you know who come here and begin interrogating them."

Forrest supposed that she was saying what was best for her. But he wondered if she was not also consciously warning him what was best for himself. It was true that the thief seemed to be someone who had watched his movements. In his own mind, there was no doubt that it was the boy who had been there the night before. And the only person whose name he could give to the police would be Marcello's.

"But what about the landlady?"

The maid, despite her unworldly air, knew exactly what to do. She went out and returned with a locksmith. The landlady, she said, should not be informed of what had happened. She should be told that he had lost his key and had the lock changed. The locksmith had finished, and was putting his tools away, when Robert appeared. The sight of him carried Forrest farther from his pre-lunch calm.

"What are you doing here?" he demanded. "I thought you were in Greece."

Robert was sunburned and heavier. His bright, self-assured air struck Forrest as unsympathetic.

"I'm in Rome for six hours," he said. "On my way to New York."

There was nothing to do but to tell him what had happened. The maid chorused Forrest's recitation of how they had repaired the door. Robert was blithely reassuring. If nothing was missing, no harm was done.

While he was there, the woman who had invited Forrest to dinner the night before telephoned. She was returning to Positano that evening. Her chauffeur would meet her in Naples and drive her the rest of the way in the car. Why didn't Forrest come with her and stay a few days?

He had refused the invitation before. This time he said yes.

CHAPTER 9

In Rome, there is no reward for the righteous, no punishment for the wicked. Payments are mixed. Despite the Church, the city has successfully confused good and evil.

The solution is ingenious. Practically everything is forbidden; therefore, practically everything is allowed; all that you need is to have the pertinacity to work out the allowed means. Eden is recreated, with the ever-present danger of picking the forbidden fruit in the wrong manner and bringing about your fall. Good and evil may be determined by the way you crook your finger when reaching out, or by the direction in which you cast your eyes. It is a solution full of good humor and deadly consequences. As soon as you have made an irrevocable choice, such as marriage, you find out which your fate is. Therefore — *quindi, dunque, poi;* the words polka-dot Italian conversation — therefore, there must always be several *therefores.*

"My father and I are not speaking," Marcello had said to Ninì, "therefore, we will not have a fight."

This way he persuaded her to come to the beach with the family on Sunday.

"Forrest has not spoken to me," Marcello said to himself at the Santa Severa station. "Therefore, if I do not speak, no one will be the wiser."

Monday morning, his father informed his mother, "The money here for your household expenses is three thousand lire short. Therefore, get three thousand from Lello."

"You did well at the school," the secretary at the office

of the parrucchiere shops told Marcello that afternoon. "But we do not have any opening now. Therefore, you will have to wait."

It was what he had expected, but it took an effort to keep his spirits up. "Come back in a month," she had added. Therefore, nothing would come of it. The middle of summer would be too late.

He had not planned to meet Ninì after work and ride home with her, but he jumped impulsively on a bus that went near Piazza Vittorio. She would be more comfort than anyone at his house.

He was told at the wholesale store that Ninì was not there. When he asked if they knew where she was, her youngest brother came out among the bundles of clothing and said no. His attitude was not friendly. Marcello took another bus home.

At the apartment, he said that the parrucchiere shop had told him that they would let him know later when he was to start work. His sisters did not question further; they were too intent on showing him the featherless baby bird that had hatched out of one of the eggs. He wondered why Ninì did not telephone him. After a while, he telephoned her. Her aunt answered. She said that Ninì could not speak to him.

"Will you ask her to call me?"

"I think it is best that you don't speak to her for a while."

"Why?"

"I think that it is best."

"Has something happened?"

"Don't insist, Marcello."

"Is Ninì all right?"

"Yes, she is all right. But I can't talk to you now. Goodbye."

He hung up, feeling miserable. What had happened? Nothing had been wrong when they had come back from Santa Severa the evening before. Her family had known that she had gone with him and his mother and father and sisters. They had been friendly at the wedding and when he had gone to the reception. Something must have happened to Ninì. But, if it had, why wouldn't they tell him?

He went back to his sisters and asked if they had seen Ninì that day or heard anything about her. But they knew no more than he did.

Just before it was time for his father to arrive home for supper, he walked past Ninì's house, hoping that he might see her. All that he saw was the red Alfa Romeo and the Giulietta Sprint.

After supper, he watched television with the others in the salon, then lay on the bed in his room, going through the help wanted ads in the Sunday *Il Messaggero.*

The next morning, he called Forrest's apartment, but there was no answer. He went to see about one of the jobs. It was taken. At midday, Claudia asked him:

"Are you going back to the school today?"

"No."

"I was hoping that you could get me another of those sample bottles of shampoo. Maybe when you're working."

He seemed left out of everything. His sisters were interested only in the baby birds; all of the eggs had hatched, and now there were three. His father seemed to have forgotten all about him. They had spoken at Santa Severa, not to fight, but calmly and about practical matters; but they had not spoken since. His father was in and out of the house all day, more than Marcello remembered his ever having been. But he was involved in making telephone calls about his business and seemed to give no thought to his son. His mother, in a pause of doing something for his father, brought a stack of his clean clothes into his room and asked him to put them away. Even she was too busy to bother with him. Nobody seemed aware that he had not seen and could not see Ninì.

The next day passed the same way. In the afternoon, he went by Forrest's apartment and rang the bell. No one answered. He took a bus that let him out near Piazza Vittorio and stood for an hour around the corner from the wholesale store, where he could see but not be seen, watching to catch sight of Ninì going in or out. He did not see her. Around eight, he took a bus back to Prati. He stood for half an hour on Viale delle Milizie, hoping to catch sight of her there. After supper, he watched television with the family again.

Thursday morning, he left the house with the want-ad pages out of *Il Messaggero*. On Viale delle Milizie, he saw Ninì's oldest brother getting into the red Alfa Romeo and asked him:

"Excuse me, do you know where Ninì is?"

"Good morning, Marcello. Yes, she went with her aunt to Palestrina for a few days."

"Why wouldn't they let me speak to her the other day?"

"Well—haven't you talked with your father?"

"With my father? Why?"

The brother looked at him narrowly. He was so large and dark that it was hard to believe he was any relation to Ninì. At last, he gave a friendly smile.

"I don't know what it is between you and your father. But he came to see me Monday and told me that he thought you and Ninì were seeing too much of each other."

"Why?"

"That's what I ought to ask you. You know what I took that to mean. The family was upset. They thought that something had happened at the beach Sunday. I'm inclined to believe Ninì and you. What have you to say?"

"My father knows that Ninì and I were always with my sisters at the beach. He just wants to make trouble for me."

"Why should a father want to do that to his son?"

"Because I don't want to work for him. I want to work somewhere else."

"I should think you'd be glad to work for your father. It's the natural thing for a son to want."

"When I do, he doesn't pay me. He wants me to work for him and then beg him for everything he gives me."

"I can see your point. He mentioned, too, that Ninì had given you a watch. That upset my aunt. She thought that you had given Ninì the money to buy it."

"I'll give the watch back to Ninì if your aunt wants me to. But it isn't right that your family should think badly of me because of my father. I don't see too much of Ninì. I am very fond of her. And I want to see her as much as I can. But you know that she works all day and that I have been going to school."

"Ninì is barely sixteen."

"I know. But she has a very mature mind."

Her brother smiled again.

"I like you, Marcello. And so does my wife. I'll see what I can do for you But, take my advice: get straightened out with your father."

When Marcello arrived home for dinner, the door was opened by Claudia, wearing a half-made dress. His father was seated in the hall, talking on the telephone.

"Ciao, Lello. Papa's looking for you. I think he wants something."

He followed Claudia to the door of his sisters' room. His aunt and mother were kneeling on the floor, fitting skirts on her and Norma.

When his father hung up the telephone, he called Marcello into the salon and closed the door. He held out an opened letter.

"This is for you. It came espresso last night."

Marcello looked down at the sheet of paper in his father's hand.

"Why did you open my letter, Papa?"

His father did not give him the letter, but held it while he read. *Out of Rome until Friday. But I know you can use this.* Between the sheet and the envelope, he could see a bank note.

"Who sent you this letter?"

"I don't know."

His father walked away, then turned abruptly back.

"You don't know anything except how to lie, do you?"

Marcello's face hardened with the effort to keep his eyes on a level with his father's.

"Nevertheless, you surprise me. This is one thing that I never expected of you."

"What?"

"Don't play the fool with me."

"I don't know what you mean."

"Liar."

Marcello smiled.

"Perhaps you think it's from Ninì."

His father threw the letter down on a table.

"There isn't any disgrace that you won't eventually bring on us, is there?"

"I haven't brought any disgrace on you. It is you who have tried to bring disgrace on me. Why did you go Monday to see Ninì's brother?"

"Leave your Ninì out of it. She has nothing to do with this."

"Why not? You complained about her giving me a watch. What do you care, Papa, where I get money, as long as it isn't from you?"

His father came toward him with his hand raised in a threatening gesture.

"I'll show you what I care. In this house you'll do as I say, or you'll get out."

"What do you say that I should do, Papa? Not get money from you, and not get it from anyone else, and pay rent?"

"Just watch your step. I'm on to you now. Think twice before you cross me again."

The telephone rang. His father picked up the letter and started out of the room. As he opened the door, Marcello said:

"I've already thought more than twice, Papa."

"Here," his father said, thrusting the letter at him. "Take it, take it!"

Marcello took it.

Forrest returned to Rome Thursday evening at nine o'clock, on a slow train that crept in past the aqueduct arches and grass grandstands of the campagna. The moon, which had seemed full all the time that he was away, rose fuller than ever over the bottle-green landscape into the sea-blue sky.

He had discovered what he had set out to discover: the problem of Rome did not exist outside of Rome, even as short a distance away as Positano.

In Positano, he had not once experienced the restlessness that he felt at Rome. He had been able to discuss the Eternal City as though it were any other trivial topic.

"The interesting thing about Rome," he had said, "is that it is comprehensible. You can know all of it. You keep discovering new things, but they are details in what you already know."

"Rome is the only city," his hostess had said, "that turns itself into people's interpretation of it. I know a woman who has had an unhappy love affair there. She insists that complete strangers come up to her on the street and whisper in her ear: Leave Rome, leave Rome!"

The woman, however, was unable to leave the city; she loved it too much.

"Do you like Rome?" a kept-looking youth who was a guest had asked him.

"Yes."

"But you are not a lover of Rome," his hostess had said. "I remember from when you came to meet the cardinal."

"I think," he had said, "that you can call me one now."

His problem had not existed while he was gone. But it was waiting for him on his return. He felt his old restlessness as he went through the streets from the station to the apartment. He had only been home a few minutes when the doorbell rang.

"Marcello, what are you doing out at this hour?"

The boy came in without answering and sat on the sofa.

"How did you manage to get away from home?" Forrest asked.

"I haven't been at home since midday."

"That's right. You've started working. How is it going?"

"No. There's no opening now. I have to wait for a job."

Forrest sat down beside him. It was nearly ten o'clock.

"Won't you get in trouble at home, staying away so late?"

"My father has put me out."

"Put you out?"

"He told me to do as he said or leave. Therefore, I left. He opened your letter."

"He put you out because of my letter?"

"No."

He explained a little to Forrest; not about Ninì, but about his father's wanting him to pay rent.

"He understood the letter completely," he added. "But that isn't why."

"I'm sorry," Forrest said. "Do you want me to give you the money to pay him rent?"

"No. He should pay for me, not you."

Forrest felt out of his depth. He put his hand on Marcello's neck and asked him what he had been doing all day.

"Looking for a job. Walking. I came by here earlier."

"Have you eaten?"

Marcello shook his head.

"Don't you have any money?"

"Yes, I have the money that you sent me."

"You mean that your father gave it to you?" Forrest exclaimed in surprise. "That's very strange. Well, aren't you hungry?"

"Yes." For the first time that evening, Marcello smiled. "Very. I ate hardly any dinner."

In the trattoria, instead of looking younger than his age, Marcello looked older. Forrest could picture him as an adult, and he realized that it was the first time he had seen Marcello doing anything except waiting or listening. He did not eat as though he were in a social situation; he ate as though he were engaged in a task. His features were the same, but they appeared less vulnerable. They expressed acceptance instead of expectation. He might be the father of a family, eating supper at the end of the day, glad to have a moment alone at the table while his wife put the children to bed. This is what he will look like at twenty-five, Forrest thought. The sparkle behind his eyes, the wondering if there is anything that life is not capable of, was replaced by a reflective wondering if, after all, this could be all. It was not a look of disappointment. The incredulity had been in his expectation; it was not in his acceptance. His expression was so sensible that he seemed incapable of becoming bitter from disappointment, and it was just this sensibleness that had always made his look of expectation so beautiful. There was no ignorance in it, no optimistic stupidity; it was clear-sighted and intelligent, and at the same time it contained complete willingness. Let life be as wonderful as it could be, he would accept it. But he waited for life to make the extravagant gestures. His own moves, however bold, were mundane. He did not consciously allow the expectation to show through his eyes. Now that its glow was absent and the features of his face lacked its luminosity, he was still handsome. But his features could be judged objectively. The intangible quality was gone. The beauty that could not be located, and therefore was marvelous, had temporarily vanished. The shape of his face, the line of his nose and jaw, were not exceptional. Yet the emotion that this realization gave Forrest was more bafflingly deep than ever. It is ordinary to love the marvelous; it is marvelous to love the ordinary.

"Listen," he said when they had finished eating. "I am going to ask you to do something for me."

He had thought of two different boys: the poor one that he had met the other night at the Spanish Steps, and the rich one, kept by a friend of his hostess, who had been introduced to him in Positano.

"What?"

"Go home now."

"I am never going home."

"Your father can probably force you to return. And if that is true, the sooner you go back the better."

"Can't I stay with you tonight?"

"You know that I would like it. But it might get us both into trouble."

"No one will know. Then I will get a job and rent a room."

"You would not like life in a room, Marcello. I assure you. No matter how unpleasant your father is to you, all the things that you like are possible because you live at home with your family."

"But my father is impossible."

"I know. But despite that, for your own sake, you must make peace with him."

Marcello looked more unhappy than ever.

"That is what Ninì's brother says," he said.

"Do they know that you have left home?"

"No."

"You will find them different if you live in a room."

When they were outside, Forrest asked:

"Which bus do you take home?"

"I am not going home."

"Come along. We'll walk. I'll go with you."

They went up the Lungotevere, past the Scalo de Pinedo, where the trees end and wide steps lead down to house-boats. The river was low and Forrest could see clusters of grass and branches on the supports of Ponte Matteotti, marking the high point that the water had reached in the spring. The bridge was deserted. On the other side, Viale delle Milizie was quiet. Marcello explained what services the different barracks belonged to, identified the school that he had attended when he was small, and pointed out the house where Ninì lived. Forrest had never heard him talk so much.

"Might we run into your father?" he asked.

"No. He will be asleep."

"Even with you missing from the house?"

"Perhaps not. But he will be in pajamas. When he is in a bad mood, he eats supper in pajamas."

They passed hedges, enclosing the outdoor tables of a restaurant. The moonlight threw their shadows on the sidewalk as sharply as the sun in the daytime, but the restaurant was dark and closed for the night. So was the pastry shop on the corner of Via Giordano Bruno. Forrest accompanied Marcello to the entrance of his house. At the door, he said:

"Remember, do not fight with your father."

"I'm not going in," Marcello said. "Walk me to my aunt's house. It is not far from here. That will be better."

Forrest accompanied him several blocks toward Saint Peter's.

"Are you sure that this is better?"

"Yes. My father and I would fight. My aunt is the best person to talk to him."

Forrest watched the empty entrance arch after Marcello had disappeared. There was no further sign of life. He walked back to Viale Giulio Cesare and waited for a bus to take him across the river.

There are not many people out in Rome late in the evening, but the streets are seldom deserted all night long. A group of youths were playing guitars among the stone lions at the base of the obelisk in Piazza del Popolo when Forrest descended from the bus. He stayed and listened. One o'clock struck before he hurried down the long straight yardstick of Via del Babuino toward home.

The telephone was ringing as he reached the apartment. He could hear it on the landing. It continued while he turned the key in the lock, which clicked five times before it opened. He almost wished that the ringing would stop before he was inside. The event which he pictured as the cause of the sound was Marcello reporting a disaster.

He pushed the seesaw light switch and hurried to the telephone. It was a long-distance call from New York.

"I know that it's late there," his wife said, "but I've been trying to reach you for two days and there's been no answer. I talked to Robert yesterday and he told me about the apartment's being broken into. I've written you. But I want to know how you are."

"I'm fine," he said. "I've been in Positano, that's all. What did Robert say to upset you?"

"Nothing, really. He just got me by chance. I've come into New York to start getting the apartment cleaned. Those people left it in an awful mess. I'm going to have it painted before we move back in. It was probably the apartment here that upset me as much as anything."

"Are you all right?"

"Yes, I'm fine. It's hot here."

"And the children?"

"They're fine. They're in the country. They miss you, too. Well, we won't run up a bill. I've written you a letter. It's just that I wanted to know how you are."

After he had hung up the telephone, as Forrest was undressing in the bedroom, he longed for the closeness and security of home, the closeness and security, that he had sent Marcello back to. He wished that he was near to his wife and children, to the things that had existed in his life before and that would continue to exist, despite the vicissitudes of love. He wanted to be where other people's need of him filled in the hiatuses in his own needs. The people who needed him were all so far from Rome. He thought of the apartment in New York, full of large and small rooms, of familiar and loved objects. The telephone conversation had given him a change in perspective. He saw himself from far away. He, too, needed much that he lacked. Opposing emotions constrained his heart. He wished that a hand would reach down out of the sky and draw together all his longings and disappointments. And as he turned out the light, he wondered if there would ever be anyone in New York with whom he would talk about Marcello.

Marcello stood in the Las Vegas Bar, waiting for Ninì and talking with a group of his friends about the difficulty of finding an agreeable job. As he talked, his thoughts remained on one fact: his father had given him the money.

The full significance of this had not struck him until Forrest mentioned it. The money had been in his father's hand, something he could have kept toward the rent he said was due. Marcello had thought that he would confiscate it and keep the letter to use against him with Ninì. But no: his father had given him the money.

The night before, when his aunt let him in, she telephoned the family and told them that he was spending the night there. He did not hear all that she said, but she spoke to his father and she mentioned Renzo. He arrived home in the morning after his father had left for the kiln. His mother and sisters greeted him with admonitions; but they were not worried. Everything was going to turn out all right. His father had agreed to forgive him if he would ask his pardon and say that he was sorry for the things he had said the day before.

"I have no intention of asking his pardon for anything," Marcello replied. "I will not fight with him, no matter what he says to me. I have promised. But I will not ask his pardon. I will not put myself in the wrong. If he wants me to be friendly, let him make a friendly move toward me."

His mother warned him and went about her work. His sisters were begging him and saying what a little thing it was to ask of him when Ninì telephoned.

"I can't talk," she said. "I don't want anyone to know that I'm calling. Meet me at one o'clock at the Las Vegas Bar."

She burst into tears as soon as they were alone together. He was downstairs with her in the ping-pong room. Only one light was lit. The music of a loud rock 'n' roll record could be heard from the jukebox upstairs. Ninì was leaning back against the edge of a table; he was standing, facing her, with his arms about her.

The tears were streaming over her cheeks; the flesh below her eyes was pale. She pressed against him. He kissed her face and neck.

"No, Marcello. We have to talk."

"Ninì, I love you."

"Marcello, someone might come."

"All right. But stop crying."

"I've been so unhappy the last four days."

"I know."

She asked him about the job at the parrucchiere shop and he told her what had happened.

"They didn't let me go back to work after dinner on Monday," she said, already beginning to be relieved by having someone to tell what she had been telling herself for days. "Then they took me to Palestrina the next morning. It was supposed to be to help my aunt with my great-aunt, who's sick. But it was as though I'd been kidnaped. The house we stayed in was like one of those hovels on Monte Mario. My room didn't have a window. And my great-aunt made awful noises all the time."

"I know. I was around old people like that when we visited Sicily."

"There wasn't anyone young there. First, my aunt talked to me as though I were a child who didn't know anything. Then she talked as though I knew a great deal more than she did and she was trying to find it out. She claimed that I'd told her that you gave me the money to buy your watch and that I must have had a reason to lie. But I hadn't told her anything. She'd just assumed that. And when we came back, my oldest brother backed me up."

She had stopped crying and dried her eyes on a handkerchief.

"It's my father," Marcello said. "He's been worse than ever since you left. Yesterday I almost left home."

"I guess he meant to do us harm," Ninì said, "but he's done us good instead. My aunt and brother will ask you to come to the house on Sunday. I'm not supposed to see you before. But I'll meet you tomorrow evening. I'm working at the workshop near here, not at the store. I'll meet you at the corner back of Piazzale degli Eroi where they're finishing the new buildings. No one will see us there."

She did not allow him to walk her home, or even out of the café. When he came upstairs, after she was gone and everyone else had left except the boy behind the bar, he played the record that he had heard while they were downstairs. Then he walked home slowly, trying to keep his spirit up with the fact that he had seen Ninì, that everything seemed to be all right, and that he had gone far enough toward meeting his father on friendly terms by promising that he would not argue. But he did not know what was going to happen. As he entered the house, he reassured himself by remembering again what he had remembered before: his father had given him the money.

The apartment door was open, as though someone were arriving or leaving. Signor Tocci was in the hall. His father greeted the older man, then they closed themselves in the salon.

Marcello wandered about the apartment and terrace, smiling at the baby birds, frowning at his sisters. He was as nervous, waiting for the encounter with his father, as he had been on the days that he had not seen Ninì. But what he expected did not happen. His father sent back word for the family to eat without him; then, when he appeared, he asked Marcello to leave with Signor Tocci and bring back some papers.

"You don't have an appointment?"

"No, Papa."

"Very well."

He went with Signor Tocci in his Fiat 1500 to an office inside a courtyard on Via Appia Antica. It was a pleasant ride, but he felt that he could have driven the automobile better than the old man did. He returned on buses to the apartment. His father took the envelope that he had brought.

"Is this all?"

"Yes, Papa."

"He didn't send any message?"

"No, Papa."

They waited, both ill at ease, unsure of the next move.

"Do you want to say something to me?" his father asked.

"No, Papa."

"Bell'arti parrari picca," his father muttered. It was a proverb in Sicilian dialect that his father liked: To speak little is a virtue.

Marcello did not know if it were meant conciliatorily or sarcastically. He waited a moment, then left the room.

"How does it go with your father?" Forrest asked when Marcello came on Saturday afternoon.

They were in the front room; Forrest was drinking a glass of vermouth, but Marcello had refused one.

"The same. No, it is better. He is too busy to fight."

"He hasn't asked you to pay rent again?"

"No. Last night at supper, he could talk of nothing but the designs for new tiles that he is going to make for a large group of buildings. I went in the afternoon and picked up the patterns for him from another kiln. Having them in his hands convinced him that he is going to have the job. I don't think that he believed it before."

Forrest watched this new Marcello with interest. He was the same and yet different. He looked like a child again; his mature transformation had not outlasted the evening; but he described his father's actions and character with an objectivity that was artful and entertaining. He was unromantic, Forrest realized; he lacked the romance of being unfeeling toward others as well as the romance of poeticizing himself. He took a clear and obvious joy in observing and describing.

Forrest had wondered during the last day if their relationship might not be different when they met again. In their conversation as he had accompanied Marcello up Viale delle Milizie, he had been given, without his asking, the confidences that he had wanted for so long. As though he were a member of the family, he had persuaded Marcello to return home, and he had been treated as a member of the family in return. Now, Marcello told him in clear, full, direct answers to his questions, all about his father's business. He explained how the clay from which the tiles were made was brought from near Naples, how the glaze was dipped on, and how the designs were applied through patterns pricked in sheets of paper. The coloring was in powdered form, and of quite different shades than it would be after it was baked. Each of these explanations sounded as though it were being created, then and there, as it was spoken. When Marcello finished, he smiled as a child smiles when he gives you a present that he has made.

Forrest reached out his hand and laid it on the nape of Marcello's neck, where he had first noticed the boy's physical combination of childishness and maturity. Forrest, too, had changed. He had not suffered his lost feeling after separating from Marcello the last time. But he, too, remained somewhat the same. His desire to touch Marcello, born of his incredulity when he had not been able to believe in this combination of traits, was calmer and deeper. But it was as strong as ever. His hand remained on Marcello's neck all the time he was listening, as though neck and hand were part of a statue, both carved from the same piece of marble, resting there lightly and forever.

Love's power is that it lets you exist outside your own body. Forrest had seen the awareness of this power raised to an almost unbearable degree in his wife when she looked at their small children. He had seen it in the children, too, long before they could have been aware of the mortal traps of their own bodies; they watched their mother leave them with the incredulity of people watching their own selves walking away from them. It is present in affection's most immaterial manifestations, in the knowledge that your thoughts contain another person, or that another person has you in his mind. Its biological end is the creation of a new body, and because of this it has been taught that the love between men should remain chaste. But life is not so clearly defined. Forrest had suffered less from an aberration of thought when he felt that a part of himself was leaving him each time with Marcello than he had suffered from a failure to accept what was happening. He accepted it now. But it did not make him chaste. He was glad when he realized that, despite the change in their relationship, and whether for money, or desire, or affection, Marcello had come to the apartment that day, as he had come in the past, with the specific intention of going to bed. Forrest's hand remained on the boy's neck as they walked into the other room. And although he had not given much subsequent thought to his drunken longing to be reincarnated as a Roman, he sensed that it was at least in part himself that he held in his arms that afternoon.

CHAPTER 10

Franco, sitting on his bed, looked questioningly at Marcello across the room.

"What is it, Franco?"

"You'll be angry with me."

"No, I won't."

Franco reached down and picked at a scab on his sunburned knee. His eyes filled with tears.

"I lost the model destroyer that you gave me. We tried to sail it at Santa Severa in the sea and it sank. I looked for it, but I couldn't find it."

"It doesn't matter."

"But you made it."

"That's all right. Perhaps Papa will buy you a kit and you can make one. Come over here and tell me what you and your little friends did after we were at Santa Severa to see you."

While Franco, sitting beside him, was telling about a trip in an open boat with the lifeguard, the door opened and their mother came into the room.

"Lello," she said, "don't leave the apartment after dinner. I want you to go with me and Franco to the tailor's."

"Why?"

"To choose material for an overcoat."

"Did Papa tell you to buy me one?"

"Does it matter?" his mother asked. She was putting away his and Franco's clean clothes. "The important thing is for you to have an overcoat next winter."

"I'm not trying to fight. I want to know whether or not to thank Papa."

"Yes, he told me to."

There had been no further mention between him and his father of the rent. A new worry had taken the place of that one. Sunday, at Nini's house, her oldest brother had offered Marcello a job for the rest of the summer, making rounds with him to retail stores and taking orders for men's shirts and socks. He would be paid a salary as well as a commission for the orders he initiated. The job was what he had wanted since he had first thought of working through the summer. That evening with Nini he had been happy.

But on his return home, and since then, he had shied at telling his father about the job and running the risk of a new fight.

"Has Papa come home?" he asked Franco.

"I don't know. I'll go and see."

He heard Franco shouting and giggling with his father and followed without waiting for him to return. At the door of his parents' bedroom, where his father kept the desk that he worked at, he stopped. As had happened several times lately, he noticed how much older his father was looking.

"May I speak to you, Papa?"

His father gave Franco a pat that sent him out of the room. Marcello, as he entered, said:

"Mamma says that I should go with her this afternoon to choose material for an overcoat." His father said nothing, and he added: "I want to thank you."

He had not decided, before he entered the room, what he was going to say. But he was suddenly aware from his father's eyes of exactly how far he could go.

"I will not be working at the parrucchiere shop this summer," he continued. "There is no opening. Is there anything that you want me to do for you?"

"You mean that you wasted the time that you went to that school?"

"Yes, I believe so."

"There are six new men working at the kiln for the last week." His father turned halfway back to his desk and picked up his pen. "I think that it is too late for you to help me now."

"I'm sorry," Marcello said. "But I do want to work this summer. You won't mind if I find a job somewhere else, will you?"

"Certainly not," his father said. "I, too, would like for you to work this summer. If you can find a job somewhere else, by all means take it."

This step toward peacefully taking the job with Nini's brother pleased Marcello. He now had three possibilities for the future: working for his father, working for Nini's family, going to sea. It also pleased him to explain to the tailor the style of overcoat that he would like. When he stopped with his mother and little brother to see his uncle on their way back, he was glad to tell his uncle about the job.

"That's good," his uncle said. "The more you know about commercial matters, the better. It will do you good to train as a salesman. Selling is important in your father's business. And no matter what you think about it now, someday your father's business will be yours."

"I doubt it. Perhaps my father wants me to work for him, but he will not want me to own his business."

"Oh, yes," his uncle said. "Sicilian families fight, but the fathers do not disinherit their sons."

"There is Franco."

"That is different. He is not the first born. This is something which you must remember in your dealings with your father. He was not a first son. That is why he left Sicily and made his way on his own. These things are important to Sicilians, and he thinks of what he has done as being for you."

"But I am not a Sicilian. I was born in Rome."

"So was I," his uncle said. "But I am a Sicilian all the same, although perhaps not quite as much a Sicilian as your father and my wife."

"I understand," Marcello said. "Perhaps I am Sicilian, too. Perhaps I am Sicilian and Roman."

"I believe so," his uncle said. "You told me the other night that your father does not understand you. But you will understand each other more all the time. You are very much alike."

Marcello smiled.

"That is what my sisters say when they are angry at me."

Forrest was not a Roman. He had to admit it as he watched the last week of his stay in Rome melt away like a block of ice in the July sun. He had become friends with the maid; she told him matter-of-factly that she prayed for him. He was one of the privileged customers at the trattoria, greeted when he entered, confided new developments in business and plans for Mauro's future. He and the storekeepers on Via della Croce spoke to each other as people do who have been acquainted all their lives. At a bar near the Pantheon, where he went for the best coffee in Rome, the men behind the counter gave him a brisk nod, as though he were a Roman, and never forgot that he did not take sugar. But he was not a Roman. He nodded to newsdealers and flower sellers; he formed a part of the Roman family that lives its life outdoors. He had less need than before to read the newspapers to know what was going on. But he still looked at *Il Messaggero* frequently, and one day he saw an item reporting the death of an American woman and her small child in an apartment near Piazza del Popolo. She had lived in Rome longer than he had. She must have been better known in her neighborhood than he was in his. Many neighbors, when they heard of the deaths, commented to the newspaper how sympathetic she and her child were. But the two of them had lain dead in their apartment for more than a month without anyone's having missed them. They were found only through the need of the electric company to read the meter. And Forrest was no more Roman than they were.

All the same, he had become better acquainted with the city; and, as the categories came back into his life, he realized that they were still lacking around him. The very space of Rome was contradictory. The narrow sidewalkless streets, when they were crowded with mobs pouring home in the evenings, gave no effect of being populated. Only later, when a handful of people were clustered together in some wide square, as the youths had been that evening beneath the obelisk in Piazza del Popolo, did the space seem inhabited.

Indoors, the rooms were nearly always odd shapes. The Roman streets rarely make right angles at corners, as the New York streets so often do; the houses follow their greater or smaller degrees and produce rooms that are neither square nor rectangular. Their shapes stimulate architects to ingenious and beautiful solutions, and illustrate how exactingly Roman life follows the facts of external reality. Curious about this phenomenon, Forrest measured the corners in the apartment one morning and found that no room had a right angle, except for the baths.

More people came to see him in the apartment. He went out with acquaintances more often. There was no longer any need for him to wander about alone, fortifying himself with the images of the green trees in Viale delle Milizie, or with the quiet fairground of the shop windows on Via Cola di Rienzo. He ate outdoors with friends in "squares" of every size and shape, in harp-shaped Largo Febo, wedge-shaped

Piazza San Cosimato, rectangular Piazza della Pigna, triangular Piazza Nicosia, and even square Piazza Santa Maria in Trastevere. These evenings dissipated his solitude and did not replace it with any equally sharp sensations. But he was glad to allow his life to flow indistinguishably back into its stream.

He had bought his airplane ticket and booked his reservation home the day that he received his wife's letter. She wrote with such intensity of her desire to be with him that he wondered if something had happened with her comparable to what had happened with him. "My life is a fragment without you," her letter said, "and you cannot live in a fragment of your own life or of someone else's." He was equally moved by her writing that their younger daughter had said a few days earlier, "I'm glad that we are going back to the city where Daddy is." Reading her letter, he thought: Perhaps it is a sin against someone you love to be interested, even in a different way, in something else. Nevertheless, in the light of such reasoning, it is for our sins that we are loved.

The painters had finished the apartment in New York. His wife was living there. She wrote of having dinner with people they knew. The children would be returning from Southport at the end of the week. The older one was to start to school. His father-in-law, now that Forrest was due back, sent him letters every day; and Forrest had talked twice on the telephone to his office. Giordano Bruno, to whom he had given no thought for a time, was officially abandoned. But Forrest had put his notes in the bottom of one of his suitcases. They were a material result of his time in Rome.

With Marcello, he had discovered that being treated as a member of the family had its disadvantages as well as its advantages. Marcello answered with a new ease when asked about his brother and sisters or about Nini's family, but he was no more willing than ever to admit himself as a subject. If Forrest asked a personal question about his thoughts or feelings, his silence was as impenetrable as before; and the "niente" with which he answered demands of what he had been doing sounded more indifferent than shy. Whatever concealed it, most that went on behind those brown Sicilian eyes was as unknown to Forrest as before. All the same, he valued the quietness that visited him those last afternoons.

The week ended dramatically. The evening before Forrest was to leave, he went to an after-dinner party with the woman who had been his hostess in Positano. The gathering was in a penthouse in Trastevere, on the river, overlooking the Isola Tiberina, the Capitoline, Palatine, and Aventine hills. The terrace across the front of the penthouse was winking with lights, like the panorama of the light-winking city. He had packed his suitcases before he went out to eat, leaving open the one with his airplane ticket and the things he would need in the morning. In the middle of the party, after several drinks, an uneasy memory came to the surface of his mind. He put a hand into his trouser pocket and pulled out his loose money.

"Do you know what it was that dropped when I was paying the taxi? It was my apartment key."

He and his friend went down to the street and searched the gutter. They questioned the old man sitting in the doorway and passersby. The key was not there and no one had seen it. They took a taxi back to his building and found the portiera, an ancient woman who was never in sight unless you looked for her. She had no key to the apartment, and when he used her telephone to call the landlady there was no answer. On a weekend in the summer she was certain to be out of Rome. He did not know her secretary's name and neither did the portiera.

"It looks as though you won't be leaving after all," his friend said teasingly. "I'll have to put you up for the night."

"The kitchen window is open and there's a ledge outside it," he told her and asked the portiera if there was a way to get to the low roof that ran across the court at the back of the building.

She thought that there was, from a building which you entered on another street. She led them around the corner and they explained their plight to another portiera. The roof of the building could be reached, she agreed, but not at night. You had to go through a private apartment. After persuasion, she informed the occupants of the apartment about his trouble. They agreed immediately and happily to let him go through their rooms to the roof.

He was led by a fat woman in a dressing gown through a series of dark rooms to an alcove where a ladder went up to the back roof. She followed him up the ladder far enough to poke her head out and direct him which way to go. His kitchen window was visible and open, but a long, narrow courtyard separated him from it. The way to cross from where he was to where he wanted to be was along a ledge that ran on the outside of a mansard roof above the street.

While the woman on the ladder shouted directions, he started across. When he was on the other side and looked down to the distant cobblestones, he was glad that he had not hesitated. The view of the street unnerved him and he was drenched in sweat. He reached the window, climbed down, and slipped in, careful not to look at the concrete court, four stories below, at the bottom of the window-lined well.

His friend was waiting for him with the portiera. He had found an extra key in the apartment and he accompanied her back to the party. But he did not stay. He preferred to return alone across Rome. He had hoped to see Marcello on his last day. But it was a Sunday; Marcello's Sundays were no more his own than they had ever been, and he had gone to the beach with his family. Earlier in the evening, before Forrest had eaten dinner, he had telephoned Marcello's house for the first time and asked to speak to him. He hoped that Marcello might find some last-minute excuse to get out of the apartment and that they might eat together. The family was back from the beach; one of the sisters answered the call; and when Marcello came to the telephone he agreed to tell his father that it was a friend who wanted him to go to a dance. He tried to get permission, but it was useless. His father refused to allow him out of the apartment after the whole day on the beach at Ostia.

Marcello had promised that he would see Forrest in the morning if it was possible. But Forrest was leaving early; he did not think that it would be. The walk across the roof ledge had been the last of his Roman adventures, and this return through Rome on foot was his farewell to the city. All around him as he walked, he sensed the physical complexity of the earth present beneath the streets and buildings. In the air there was an atmosphere of Paradise, not of perfection but of all things being possible. He was trying to go in a more or less straight line, rather than through the larger and more frequented streets, and he became lost in an obscure byway. He could find neither lights, nor people, nor an open space. Then, suddenly, he came but into a small, dark, deserted square, in the center of which, lit by a spotlight, was the fountain of the tortoises. By some chance, he had never seen it before. He stood looking at the figures of the four youths, enclosed between the scallop shells below and the round, umbrella-like basin above, their hands raised in gestures that were neither of greeting nor farewell, but of support to the small creatures at their finger tips. In the midst of his surprise, a joy leapt up in Forrest's heart. He walked on, glad that he had been in Rome and glad that he was returning home. Such sights and such feelings are not isolated in Rome. A few moments later, he discovered in Largo Argentina the value of fragments and the wisdom of keeping them separate. The city was his. He passed almost no one all the way to the apartment. He reached the house, mounted the four flights of steps, clicked the key in the lock five times, flicked the seesaw light switch, went the round-about way to the bedroom, and turned on the weak lamp beside the bed.

Marcello woke as the sun was rising. The rest of the house was asleep. He dressed quietly, without opening the shutters and without waking Franco. He closed the door with a click when he left their room and crept up the hall. As he was opening the front door, he heard a sound from his parents' bedroom. Either his mother or father was getting up. He was willing to risk having trouble later, but he did not want to be caught now. He let himself quickly out of the apartment. Instead of waiting for the elevator, he ran down the stairs.

No one was on the street. Behind the parked automobiles, the shutters of the stores were locked. Everything was dusty in the early morning light. But there were a number of people on the bus when it came. He found a seat on the right side and watched Ninì's house as it passed. Yesterday at the beach, away from the others in a stretch as deserted as the streets were now, he and Ninì had made love. There had happened between them what had not happened when they met at the guard's shack behind the newly completed buildings beyond Piazzale degli Eroi. He thought of it as he rode. He had been more timid than she was. For the first time in his encounters with sex, the vulnerability of another person had frightened him. Of all the magics he had encountered, this was the least easy to hold in his mind. And, as the bus carried him to see Forrest, he thought with longing of proving his experience with Ninì again.

A waiter was banging up the shutter of a latteria, a woman was opening the window of a newspaper kiosk, where he descended from the bus. A boy with a tray of pastries on his head stopped his bicycle in front of Marcello and carried the pastries into an open bar. He followed the boy inside, drank a cappuccino, ate a maritozzo, and went on. Life was beginning, also, on the street where Forrest lived. Trucks turned toward the market on Via Bocca di Leone; drivers shouted to one another.

Forrest, who had gone to sleep to the sound of cats making love, woke up to the sound of slamming automobile doors. He was lying in bed, listening to the early morning rattle of traffic, so like the early morning rattle of traffic at Seventy-Second Street and Central Park West, when the doorbell rang. He answered it in his robe. He and Marcello returned to the bedroom and, sitting on the unmade bed, Forrest recounted his adventures of the night before. Marcello said nothing of what he had done on Sunday. He told, instead, his plans for the day. At nine o'clock, he was to meet Ninì's brother at the wholesale shop. They would start out in the brother's automobile. He would have a case of samples and go to some stores with the brother. Then he would go to other stores on his own.

"You ought to shave," Forrest said.

"I shaved Saturday. I only shave twice a week."

"From now on, perhaps, you should shave three times a week. Here, you can use my electric razor."

When Marcello had finished, Forrest took the razor and went over his face again. As he did, he placed his free hand on the nape of Marcello's neck and said:

"I am going to miss you."

Marcello knew that they were going to miss each other, but he made no reply. He had nothing to say about it. There was no point in talking about a thing that was known and could not be changed. Any feeling could be turned into words; on occasions this was the right thing to do. But there was nothing for him to say to Forrest about these feelings. An obscure difference separated what he could say to one person from what he could say to another, and since yesterday fewer words than ever seemed useful between him and Forrest. The silence lasted until Forrest laughed.

"Perhaps you are an angel," he said, "but you have feathers of stone."

Forrest dressed and closed his suitcase.

"Very well," he said. "Let's go. Help me with these things."

Marcello carried one of the suitcases. He waited while Forrest found the portiera and gave her the key.

They caught a taxi to the station. The drive carried them through the Villa Borghese, beautiful in the early morning light. Now that summer had come, and the capers, and orange trees, and magnolias, and even the pomegranates had bloomed, the mimosa was out again. Marcello remembered that it had been blooming when they first walked together in the Villa Borghese. He knew that it would please Forrest for him to mention this, the same way that it would please Forrest for him to say that he would miss him. But he remained silent.

At Via Giolitti, they went into the airport transportation terminal and Forrest checked his luggage. Then they walked out to the sidewalk beside the bus. There was a confusion of porters, hawkers, bus drivers, passengers.

Forrest held out his hand.

"Arrivederci."

Marcello shook the hand that Forrest held out. Then he took the American by the shoulders and kissed him on each cheek, as Italians do their close friends and relatives.

"Arrivederci."

He did not smile as he stood watching the bus drive away.

Printed in January 2023
by Rotomail Italia S.p.A., Vignate (MI) - Italy